SEMBENE OUSMANE, born in Senegal in 1923, started
earning his living as a fisherman, aged 15. Essentially self-
educated, he then moved to Dakar and at the outbreak of
World War II was drafted into the French army, where he saw
action in Italy and Germany. After the war, he returned to
Senegal, but with awakening political and literary ambitions he
went to France and found work as a docker in Marseilles. He
became trade-union leader of the dockers, and until Senegal's
independence in 1960 was a member of the French Communist
Party.

Le Docker Noir, his semi-autobiographical first novel, appeared
in 1956, and reflects Ousmane's experiences in Marseilles. Since
then, his literary output has been prolific, with *Oh Pays, mon
Beau Peuple!*, *Les Bouts de Bois de Dieu*, *Voltaïque*, a collection of
short stories, and *L'Harmattan* appearing in rapid succession.
The latter opened up a new avenue in his career, prompting an
invitation to study at the Moscow film school in 1964. A prize
at the Venice film festival in 1973, for the film of his short story
Le Mandat, earned him an international reputation as a director.
In 1973 the novel *Xala* was published, and made into a
successful film. Ousmane's latest novel appeared in 1981 – a
major, two-volume work, *Le Dernier de l'Empire*.

Heinemann's African Writers Series also includes the following
works by Sembene Ousmane, in translation: *Les bouts de Bois de
Dieu* as *God's Bits of Wood*; *Le Mandat suivi de Véhi Ciosane ou
Blanche Genèse* as *The Money Order with White Genesis*, *Xala*, *Le
Dernier de l'Empire* as *The Last of the Empire*, and *Le Docker Noir* as
Black Docker.

SEMBENE OUSMANE

NIIWAM AND TAAW

HEINEMANN

Heinemann International Literature and Textbooks
a division of Heinemann Educational Books Ltd
Halley Court, Jordan Hill, Oxford OX2 8EJ

Heinemann Educational Books Inc
361 Hanover Street, Portsmouth, New Hampshire, 03801, USA

Heinemann Educational Books (Nigeria) Ltd
PMB 5205, Ibadan
Heinemann Kenya Ltd
Kijabe Street, PO Box 45314, Nairobi
Heinemann Educational Boleswa
PO Box 10103, Village Post Office, Gaborone, Botswana

LONDON   EDINBURGH   MADRID
PARIS   ATHENS   BOLOGNA   MELBOURNE
SYDNEY   AUCKLAND   SINGAPORE
TOKYO   HARARE

First published by Heinemann International Literature
and Textbooks in the African Writers Series in 1992
Series Editor Adewale Maja-Pearce

Translated by a team from the Department of French Language
and Literature (post-graduate research programme), University
of Cape Town, comprising Gioia Eisman, Catherine Gleen-Lauga,
Nadine Pienaar, Anny Wynchank, with the participation of
Lynn Scholtz, Masters student in Literary Studies

British Library Cataloguing in Publication Data

Ousmane, Sembene
Niiwam and Taaw. – (African writers series)
I. Title   II. Series
843 [F]

ISBN 0435 906712

Printed and bound in Great Britain by
Cox & Wyman Ltd, Reading, Berkshire

92 93 94 95 10 9 8 7 6 5 4 3 2 1

Contents

Preface

SEMBENE OUSMANE, VOICE OF THE VOICELESS

Born in Dakar, Senegal, in 1923, Sembene Ousmane is a unique phenomenon on the African artistic scene. He received no formal education after completing the primary school *Certificat d'Etudes*, but he supplemented this lack with wide reading and, self-taught, has become one of the world's most widely read and translated African authors. His itinerary has been remarkable: before becoming a celebrated and famous film producer, he followed the most varied occupations – he was a fisherman in Haute Casamance (Senegal) and a plumber, mechanic and bricklayer in Dakar. In 1942 he joined the French colonial army and fought in Africa and Europe. In 1948, he embarked clandestinely for France, and worked as a stevedore and docker in Marseilles. There, he participated in several trade union demonstrations and joined the Communist Party in 1950. His first novel, *Le Docker Noir*, was published in 1956. That same year an accident, which resulted in a spinal fracture, immobilised him for some months in Denmark and allowed him to reflect deeply on his own principles and on the social problems of his people. He realised how important it was for him to seek and express his African identity. Back in Paris, after travelling in the USSR in 1957, he regularly met the leftist intelligentsia: Jean-Paul Sartre, Simone de Beauvoir, Paul Eluard, Aragon, and Black writers such as Aimé Césaire, Léon Damas, Camara Laye, Mongo Béti, Bernard Dadié and Ferdinand Oyono. He was inspired by reading the saga *Les Thibault*, and later, meeting its author, Roger Martin du Gard. This contact proved crucial for the writer's literary evolution.

On his return to Africa, while travelling in Mali, Niger, the Ivory Coast and the Congo, he realised what little influence African literature had within its own continent. He had been a great lover of the cinema from a very early age and it seemed to him this medium was a more effective instrument to reach the people and deliver a message. 'For me,' he later said in an interview published in *Jeune Cinéma*, 'the cinema is an instrument of political action.' He tried in vain to obtain financial help for his film-making from French, Canadian, American, Polish and Czech film companies. Only the USSR answered his call. He was invited to study in the Gorki Studios, where he worked with Marc Donskoi and Sergei Guerassimov. While engrossed in film-making, he continued writing.

The subjects of Sembene's works of fiction reflect both chronologically and geographically his own life and ideological orientations. Also, from *Black Docker* (1956), to *God's Bits of Wood* (1960), *Xala* (1971) and *The Last of the Empire* (1981), one can trace his continuous creative evolution, leading through years of apprenticeship to literary maturity.

His early novels are concerned also with general social issues to which individual situations are subservient. *Le Docker Noir* (1956) tells the tragic adventure of the African docker Diaw Falla in Marseilles and describes his miserable life and the deplorable existence of Black workers there in the early fifties. No other novelist was better prepared than Sembene to depict the plight of expatriate African workers: precarious work conditions, frequent unemployment, inadequate wages, the lack of trade union support, the high rate of work-related accidents, incidence of sickness, etc. For Sembene, the importance of his novel lay in its message, and he addressed his book to French readers. Indeed, 85 per cent of the Senegalese public was then illiterate and those who could read, 'did not read books written by an African', as Sembene complained at the 'Dakar Conference' in 1963. In this novel, Sembene's technique reflects his interest in films and anticipates his eventual involvement in the cinema.

Sembene's second novel, *O Pays, Mon Beau Peuple!* (1957), is set in a remote fishing village in Senegal, reminiscent of the place where he spent his youth. It is again an ideological work and is recognised as the first Franco-African novel dealing with the problem of social prejudices; in terms of the rejection of a

European wife by her husband's African community, contrasting with the stereotyped rejection of blacks by whites. However, in this novel, as in *Black Docker*, the characters are not very convincing, because their actions are determined by the writer's ideology and are not psychologically motivated. The hero, the young, idealistic and dynamic Oumar Faye, comes back to his native land after fighting in the Second World War. Married to a young French girl, Isabelle, he arrives intending to awaken his country from its long slumber and stimulate its economic development. Oumar obstinately refuses to bend before the capitalistic businessmen, for he wants to found a model cooperative farm. He struggles against the colonists while simultaneously trying to shake off his compatriots' indifference and resignation, in particular that of the Elders, who do not feel any need for change.

Whereas Sembene's first two works are centred on a single hero, the horizon widens in the next novels, for the writer embraces the collective destiny of West Africa and presents a vast fresco swarming with characters. Sembene's genius blossoms with epic subjects. In *God's Bits of Wood* (1960), he receives his literary maturity and shows a greater mastery of the French language than in his first works. The novel is an historical document relating to a labour dispute that occurred in 1947 – the strike of the Dakar-Niger railway workers – told through fictional characters. It is both a story of great human appeal and a social statement, showing the sufferings of the workers and their families as a result of strike actions. The title refers to a local superstition that, by counting or enumerating people, their lives are shortened. Therefore pieces of wood are counted in place of people. The title is all the more symbolic as, contrary to the respect and the sacred value granted human beings in African thought, in *God's Bits of Wood*, the human being is jeered at, dehumanised and trampled by his fellow man. Yet Sembene's work ends on an optimistic note, for a few of the strikers' demands will be met. In spite of the suffering and loss of life, working together for the common good has been rewarding for some of the characters. Sembene handles the psychological aspects of his numerous

characters very sensitively. He avoids the temptation of presenting his whites as ogres, caricatures or stereotypes, or of idealising
his Africans. This novel pictures a class struggle rather than a
racial conflict.

Sembene's fourth novel, *L'Harmattan* (1963), is situated in an
unnamed African country, which represents a number of West
African states at the time of de Gaulle's referendum of 1958. The
novel evokes the crucial stages of the struggle for self-determi-
nation just before the dawn of independence in the sixties. The
title is suggestive: the *Harmattan* is a hot, dry wind blowing
everywhere in West Africa from the east or north-east, between
December and March. This wind is symbolic of the spirit of
independence and freedom that was blowing across the black
Continent in the fifties, clearing away injustice, corruption and
superstition as obstacles to progress. For Sembene, the only hope
for the future lay in unquestioning observance of the principles of
African socialism.

Xala (1971) gives a picture of post-independence society in
Senegal. It is a satire of the greedy bourgeoisie, the *nouveaux riches*
who acquired their wealth through dishonesty and deceit. This
novel, written with much humour, demonstrates a keen obser-
vation of the contemporary African urban society.

Finally, Sembene's last novel, *Le dernier de l'Empire* (1981),
published in English as *The Last of the Empire*, relates a consti-
tutional coup perpetrated by the President of the Republic of
Senegal. It underlines, sometimes with grating humour, the
antagonism between the partisans of neocolonialism who become
aware of the failure of their policy, and the power-hungry
nationalists of the Second Generation of Independence. This
work, more so than the others, is characterised by the cinemato-
graphic technique of the author: brief scenes in which one of the
principal characters is highlighted follow one another in short
chapters. Also, the cinema-like cutting from one scene to another
suggests simultaneous action.

The same technique and the same talent are apparent in
Sembene's short stories. In *Voltaïque* (1962), a collection of twelve

short stories, translated into English as *Tribal Scars and other stories* (1974), his art remains at its peak, as it does in two other novellas, *Vehi-Ciosane (White Genesis)* (1964), and *Le Mandat (The Money Order)* (1964), which won the literary prize at the Dakar Festival.

The two stories translated in this volume, *Niiwam* (1976) and *Taaw* (1986), plunge the reader into the world of poverty and unemployment of Dakar and describe the people's struggle for survival and dignity. In these novellas, as in his previous works, one senses Sembene's feminist stand, and his deep understanding of and love for the poor.

Sembene made *Taaw* into a film in 1970. Indeed, the scenarios of many of his films were drawn from his written works: *Niaye* (1941) was produced from *Vehi-Ciosane*, *La Noire de . . .* (1966) from *Voltaïque*, *Mandabi* (1968) from *Le Mandat* and finally, the film version of *Xala* was produced in 1975. It is significant that Sembene turned to Wolof in his later films; he wanted to ensure that he would reach the people with whom he wanted contact.

Currently, Sembene, still living in Dakar, is mostly engaged in directing and producing films, in a modest studio and usually on a very small budget. His latest film, *Le Camp de Thiaroye* (1988), depicts an infamous episode which marked the history of the French colonial army – its brutal treatment of African soldiers at the end of the Second World War.

In his films as in his written works, Sembene's driving concern has been to denounce hypocrisy, stupidity and injustice, as well as to expose the consequences of ignorance, superstition, and fatalistic passivity. His goal has always been to restore a sense of honour and dignity in the poor and the exploited of Africa and this is well illustrated by these short stories, *Niiwam* and *Taaw*.

Anny Wynchank

Commentary on the Translation

Sembene Ousmane is an African Senegalese writer. Like many of his other books, *Niiwam* is written in French and was published by the prominent publisher of African writing in Paris, France, Présence Africaine. Such details about the book are of concern to the translator.

Many have argued that the task of the translator is to trigger in the reader of the translated text responses which are similar to the responses of the reader of the original text. The question of the public which the original text addresses is therefore legitimate. What readers is a Senegalese writer aiming to reach when he writes in French?

It is generally agreed that only 20 per cent of the Senegalese population is literate in French. Sembene Ousmane himself estimates that only 10 per cent of those 20 per cent are potential readers of his books. The playwright Cheik Aliou Ndao wonders whether a percentage of 2 per cent literate Senegalese would not be a more accurate figure. Clearly, the Senegalese writer writing in French is not writing for a local audience. Locally most people cannot read at all, or cannot reach French, and have precious little income to devote to books. Like his fellow African writers, Sembene Ousmane is writing in a European language to be read beyond the borders of his country. When we translate his text into English we contribute to this endeavour by making the text accessible to many other readers in English-speaking Africa and in the English-speaking world generally.

On the other hand, like many other Africans, Sembene Ousmane feels that his African human, social and political milieu is and must be what the writer feeds on and what he must give expression to. The titles, especially *O Pays, Mon*

Beau Peuple!, and even more dramatically the books with titles in Wolof like *Xala* or *Niiwam*, bear witness to this commitment. The question facing the translator is whether the contradiction or tension between the stuff the books are made of and French, the foreign idiom in which their Africanness is couched, can be felt in the original text, and if so, how to reflect it in the translation. Pierrette Herzberger-Fofana's recent interviews of African writers, many of them Senegalese, show such contradictions are felt by the writers. Several of them express their frustration at being unable to write in their mother-tongue, which they often haven't learnt how to write, and which the majority of the population would not be able to read. They call for a linguistic policy which will promote African languages in education, political life and employment and enable their countrymen to be addressed by literature in their mother or national tongues.

Under Léopold Senghor's eminent and erudite guidance, Senegal opted for French as its official language, which Senghor believed would enable the African country to be part of the modern world of Science and international exchange. Among the seventeen African languages spoken in Senegal, six were selected as 'national languages' to be used as the medium of instruction in the first two years of primary school. But the government has implemented the policy with extreme caution; it remains at an experimental stage and the Senegalese tend to prefer sending their children to schools inherited from the French model, opening possibilities of social promotion and eventually political, administrative and economic power. Taaw and his mother Yaye Dabo see the French school as the door to employment in computers. Dropping out of school is the rule, with only one pupil reaching tertiary education out of 1000 children who started school at age seven. Along the way, things have gone wrong, with the result that children are proficient neither in Wolof nor in French and, to quote Sembene again, in urban areas youths speak a 'bastardized language' which no one understands except fellow drop-outs. They are thus sure candidates for unemployment and juvenile delinquency. Taaw's friends are explicitly identified by their sociolect; mixing French, English and Wolof. The issue of the African languages and their status versus official French is a thematic element in both short stories, as it is in *Xala*, for instance, where the young daughter of the impotent protagonist actively participates in the promotion of Wolof at university through the publication of texts translated into Wolof. Sembene himself, in 1971, contributed to a Wolof monthly publication, *Kaddu*, which did not survive the political controversy about the proper way of transcribing the language. A more recent venture, *Ande Sopi*, has also run into difficulties.

Senegal is in a more favourable position than many other African countries to undertake the development of a national language, from which, among other advantages, a national literature could emerge: 80 per cent of the population speak Wolof either as a mother tongue or as the *lingua franca*. Wolof has the further advantage of being largely spoken in Gambia as well. With many others Sembene Ousmane is calling for the political choice that will allow all Senegalese to be schooled, and therefore to read and operate economically, in the language they speak. They would be spared the linguistic violence of having to learn the basic skills of reading and writing in a foreign idiom. He remarks bitterly that the promotion of African languages runs against the interests of the French language, which is trying to resist English with the forces of 'La Francophonie', the French-speaking world. In the meantime, with 80 per cent of illiterate Senegalese associating Wolof or their mother tongue with tradition, especially oral tradition, what is the writer to do? In Sembene's novel *L'Harmattan*, Leye is a writer as well as a political militant. He decides to stop writing, in spite of a previous collection of poems which was a great success in Africa, and was translated into numerous vernaculars. His reason: he will not 'enrich the French language any more'. He turns to painting instead.

Clearly, Sembene Ousmane has made a different choice. For his African public, he writes the dialogues of his films in Wolof, but he has not given up using French. It is of crucial importance to the translator to assess whether, in his own words, he is 'enriching' French, or to know how he is using the language.

One must stress that French spoken in Africa differs quite considerably from metropolitan or standard French. The translator can use well-documented studies and lexicons recording the Africanisms. One study is devoted to specifically Senegalese usage of over 1000 lexical units, and further studies identify borrowing from various vernaculars. Wolof is the major lender, and most borrowings predictably pertain to social phenomena unknown to Europeans and nameless in French. Quite often, but not systematically, Sembene's French text is footnoted to enlighten the non-African reader. The translator is likely to translate the meaning of such units and keep authorial footnotes, and to add a glossary of Africanisms.

On top of such recorded or signalled Africanisms, the writer is at liberty to use unrecorded or personal departures from standard French. In the French text of *Taaw* a number of words appear in inverted commas. The word or phrase is usually easily understandable, but the typography acknowledges the departure from common usage. It is a challenge to the translator to find an English equivalent that will be understandable while departing from standard usage. When we translate '*son á côté*' by 'his next-door', we resort to an unusual way of saying 'his neighbour', but we do not reflect the innovative use of the French phrase, which may be regional, or a transcoding from a vernacular, or Sembene's coinage.

Sembene is very aware of the constraints of French. At times, the metropolitan reader is surprised to see such zealous use of the grammar he was taught at school; imperfect subjunctive and participial clauses have long fallen into disuse in everyday French, and in much of the written 'literary'

French. Such overcorrectness is particularly striking when it expresses the inner train of thought of Thierno, who has not been taught and does not speak, let alone read, French. But one may suggest that Sembene's written French in such cases reflects, possibly ironically, the dangerous rigid French of a Senegalese literate and political élite, keen to show their mastery of the idiom in which they were schooled. Narrative passages, especially when they rely on a highly western technique, like free reported speech, are an opportunity for Sembene to ape and mock the French-speaking African intellectual.

More frequently, however, Sembene is striving to render a more Africanized idiom. Within the morphosyntactic constraints of French, he has the reader sense the polyglossic quality of speech in Senegal. He often tags the language used by his protagonists in their utterances: 'he said in Wolof'; 'he continued in French'. In *Taaw*, a woman is reported to have uttered obscene words of abuse in her mother tongue, while the rest of her speech is reported to be in Wolof. Eventually standard and even Senegalese French burst at the seams with the language the people speak: ritualized forms of address, and social exchanges in Wolof society are transcoded with due tribute to French syntax, but the pragmatic use of language is deliberately kept foreign. Transcoding also occurs from Arabic when the text expresses prayers. Eventually Wolof words which are not recorded Senegalese French borrowings do creep in. Occasionally Sembene will footnote; elsewhere he will give the transcoding between brackets, or merely juxtapose it to the Wolof word or phrase. The reader is left to decide whether the protagonist utters both, or whether translation is provided for his convenience. At times, there is no footnote, no translation, bracketed or not; just 'Reek' or 'Tchim' or 'Deeded' giving the pale written reflection of the actual speech of Sembene's countrymen when they express disapproval, contempt, surprise or any other emotion.

Sembene willingly translates such interjections or phrases

when asked. But in such situations the translator's task is not to translate meaning, which is often clear enough from the context, but humbly to retain the words, the very letter of the text. Necessarily, the names of the protagonists are African names. Although some help is provided for Taaw, the first born, for instance, the reader ignorant of Wolof is excluded from the onomastic network. When questioned on this point, Sembene was predictably adamant that we should respect proper names. He refused to offer any equivalent for Niiwam as the text offers for Taaw and explicitly forbade the use of a subtitle.

Proper names have singular references, and as such are 'outside language', belonging to the encyclopaedia, not the dictionary. In a French text studded with 'foreign' units, one cannot always immediately distinguish the proper names from the foreign common names, or interjections. In his endeavour to orchestrate the heterogeneity of Senegalese voices, idioms and tongues within the European medium he uses, Sembene impregnates French with the irresistible force of proper, untranslatable names. The tour de force lies in his assessment of the degree of tolerance of French for such African foreign-ness: the purist of course will balk at the ruggedness of the text with the incongruous mixture of polished grammar, African neologisms, Wolof and Arabic words or turns of phrases, transcoded proverbs and metaphors. The text does not read smoothly. The cultural shock of various customs, sometimes explained, sometimes not, is accepted as anthropological curiosity. The real estrangement lies in the linguistic experience of the foreign-ness of French when used by an African.

It is very tempting indeed to seize the opportunity of translating to re-Europeanize the text and give it the smooth flow of standard literary prose, which will spare the reader of the translation the linguistic shock. The opposite strategy consists in attempting to respect the foreign-ness of the original text, without sparing the reader of the English text what a fellow translator has called 'the test of foreign-ness'. There would be no point in having the young unemployed talking the idiom of their counterparts on the Cape Flats or in Harlem, or in proposing the English transcoding of Xhosa or Zulu traditional forms of address, or ritualized social intercourse. Our effort should rather tend to reflect as much as possible the tensions, especially the linguistic tensions, that give the original text its African Senegalese life.

It may well be that the babelized idiom of the original text voices the confusion of the colonized estranged from their mother-tongue and their resistance to parroting the imperial language. The English text will serve the purpose of a translation if it gives readers some sense that their mother-tongue can open and welcome other voices and other tongues.

Catherine Glenn-Lauga

Niiwam

A T THE FOOT OF THE ROCKY CLIFF, THE calm sea was sparkling. The air was filled with different sounds: a boat's siren in the distance, the bugle calls of the soldiers doing drill in the nearby barracks, the hum of engines.

Vultures were gliding high in the sky. The day was clear and bright.

The west wing of the Aristide-le-Dantec Hospital, more commonly known as the 'Native Hospital', as a hangover from colonial times, was silent. Opposite the gaping doorway stood a hearse blocking the entrance.

Normally as one passed the morgue, one would only glance inside furtively, silently. One would of course only ever go there, at the last minute and as seldom as possible, to bury a relative, a friend, or the friend of a friend.

Men wearing either European or Senegalese clothes were standing around in small groups, or sitting on cement benches, in cars, or on the red clay ground. They chatted and smoked together, occasionally glancing over at the gate. These men, who had become so preoccupied by the various daily activities of a new Africa, and had been separated from one another by the exigencies of urban life, would come together there to renew and strengthen the ancient tradition of the *veillées*.*

Two hired buses, and cars lined up like the carriages of a train, were parked outside.

A group of people emerged from the morgue, threading their way along the narrow path left by the hearse. The woman – the only woman – appeared first. She wore simple clothes, and had tears coursing down her flat cheeks. She was followed by her

* Translator's note: mourners' vigil around a dead body.

husband, Thierno, who was carrying their dead child. A third man, well on in years, brought up the rear. He was the ragman, and clutched a large, neatly folded bag under his right arm. He was wearing a patched-up two-piece suit. He had a cap on his head, its tassel trailing over his shoulder. He seemed at ease, untroubled by the people around him. He looked at them all without embarrassment or awareness, more accustomed to the city than his companion.

'Move forward,' the ragman murmured gently but firmly in the other's ear.

Thierno obeyed, overcome by grief.

They left the woman alone. Tears were still streaming from her eyes, but she made no sound. She twisted her fingers nervously, and bit her lip. It was not physical pain that she felt. She watched her husband moving off with their only child, the old man at his side.

The people gathered there for another funeral were astonished by what they saw.

Thierno, as upright as a tree trunk, carried his son's body as if it were so much well-ironed linen. He wore a long shirt of faded blue cotton, and plastic sandals. His hardened heels were the colour of ash, and lined with deep cracks. His close-cropped hair looked like pepper-corns.

The two men did not speak. Just beyond the Pasteur Institute, they stopped to let some cars pass. The ragman, in a fatherly gesture, held Thierno's elbow to help him across the road.

At the bus stop men and women on their way back from seeing the doctor or visiting their sick in hospital early that morning, were waiting under the shelter for the bus. The old ragman had deliberately chosen this stop, second on the line, because the inspector's checkpoint was some four hundred metres away. Thierno and he, both silent, were a good distance away from the others.

● ● ●

The old ragman had met Thierno that morning. He was a regular around the morgue, for professional reasons: he used to wash the corpses so that he could have their clothes, buying them either from the warden or from the relatives of the deceased. He washed the clothes and then sold them in the suburbs of Dakar or in the country.

While waiting for his son's body, Thierno had noticed him speaking to the warden. He had gone up to them, and asked the ragman, with the utmost circumspection, leaving his sentence unfinished, 'Is it far ...?'

'What?'

The harshness of this reply threw Thierno. He was apprehensive.

The three of them stared at one another. The warden took this opportunity to give Thierno his form authorising the removal of a corpse, and went off. With his piece of yellow paper in hand, Thierno diffidently made his enquiries.

'I wonder where the cemetery is?'

'At Yoff.'

'Which is the shortest way to get there on foot?'

For a long while the ragman stared at him in disbelief, thinking: 'He's mad! There are too many madmen in Dakar.'

Thierno was distraught. 'I have to bury my son.'

At this, the old man examined him more closely. He had seen and heard a good deal since he had been in this business, but such a question, never.

'Where are you from?' he asked.

'Me?'

'Who else do you think I'm talking to? Where are you from?'

'I come from ...'

From his accent, the old man could tell that he was 'fresh from the village'.

'Do you have any money?'

'Why?' Thierno asked, suspicious. He thought for a few minutes. 'In the village, you don't need money to bury someone.'

'Things are different in the village! Here in Ndakarru*, you can't get to the cemetery without money. The cemetery is very far. It's in the village of Yoff ... To get there, you need transport. And without money, no one will take you there. Have you got money?'

Thierno shook his head. His naïveté made the ragman want to laugh. But it was neither the time nor the place. He stared at Thierno, until his attention was drawn to the woman lying prostrate in a corner near the entrance. The woman had grown used to the smell of formalin and incense, but even so the stench of decomposing matter was strong. The ragman was suddenly overwhelmed by a feeling of condescension towards them. 'Poor simpletons from the bush.' he thought.

'Have you got fifty francs?'

'Not a *sou*,' Thierno replied frankly.

The old man began to get annoyed. He wanted to just dump him there and get on with his own business, but the woman's sobs held him back.

'These peasants are trying to have me on,' he muttered. He felt a surge of pity for them, but was still quite sceptical:

'You don't have even one *centime*?'

'Yallah is my witness! Since yesterday, we haven't had a thing to put in our stomachs, her and me. We spent the night here. You can ask the warden.'

The ragman had discovered someone poorer than himself. As they were brothers in the faith, he decided to help him. He would pay the 'transport'. It was not the first time a needy person would be using public transport to go and bury a corpse. He knew the route of the number eight bus by heart.

• • •

* Translator's note: Dakar

The bus arrived.

The ragman climbed on first to buy the ticket. They were the last passengers to get on.

From the moment his feet touched the boards, Thierno could feel himself becoming more and more tense. He was gripped by fear, which grew and grew in him.

His sad eyes scanned the travellers jostling one another to find places. The dread of being discovered with Niiwam, his dead child, paralysed him.

The old ragman slipped a ticket between his fingers and nimbly jumped down after whispering in his ear,

'Go and sit down ... over there.'

Thierno took one step. But had he really moved? He bumped into the step and started. A sticky, bitter saliva filled his mouth. His eyes – for a split second – met those of the conductor. Fear stripped him of every faculty, leaving him with only a growing sense of guilt. It incapacitated him. The blood was pounding in his ears, his body was drenched with sweat. He clenched his teeth, and dared not ask for help. With no support from anyone around him, he felt like an abandoned orphan, friendless and alone, without protection, a deserted wreck. At this moment, he wished he could feel the weight of his community around him. A ward without a guardian! Did he feel that he had broken some rule? Remorse? Guilt? That he had violated a taboo? He looked dazed and terrified, and felt as though he was suffocating. He examined the ticket he was clasping between two fingers and turned around to see the old ragman, his elder. He was appealing to him again for help.

The ragman was watching him from outside the bus. He could not go with him. He had living children and two wives to feed. He had given away his entire fortune that day, fifty francs. With that amount, he could have bought a quarter of a kilogram of rice for his family. And had he not given him that old sheet to use as a shroud for his son? He could have got three to four hundred francs for that cloth. So the old man convinced himself there was nothing more he could do.

He made a sign to Thierno to move forward.

Thierno glanced in horror at the conductor, his legs unsteady under the load weighing him down. He looked down at the floor, like a small boy being scolded.

The old man had put his bag down on the pavement and with discreet gestures was trying to encourage Thierno to move forward. He moved forward too, at the same pace as Thierno. Had the ragman not been there Thierno would have got off with Niiwam, but the older man's presence kept him from taking his own decision. Three times Thierno thought of turning back, of giving up. But he knew that the older man would not let him now that he had come this far. Would he have been capable of such an undertaking all alone?

Urged on by his elder, Thierno obeyed the old man's gesticulations.

He walked past two rows, and sat down with his load on his lap. Suddenly he was filled with a feeling of peace and security. An expression of deep calm appeared in his eyes.

The old man gave him a compassionate smile. He wanted to give him moral support until the bus left, and watched him through the window.

Thierno had a commonplace face; it was bony, his eyes sunk in deep sockets under bushy eyebrows. His mouth was framed by two dark lines.

They stared at each other. Thierno closed his eyes. When he opened them again, a tear was trickling down from the corner of his eye. The ragman shook his head as if to say 'When you're a man you don't cry.' He was struggling to keep a brave front, himself, and fought back his tears.

The bell rang, the sign for the driver that it was time to leave. The one hundred and sixty horses rattled into life.

The ragman nodded his head by way of goodbye. He was not displeased with himself. He had helped other people in this way before.

The bus climbed the slope towards the water tower, heading for the centre of town. It was going to cross Dakar, from one side to the other.

Thierno paid no attention to the activity in the streets. A man or a woman would catch his eye for a few seconds, but then just as quickly the image would dissolve. Now and then the sun's rays played over him. His thoughts were whirling in his head: he could not control them, bring them to order. He buried deep into the void inside himself, where his disordered thoughts ran wild. There was nobody to guide him. In the village, whatever he did had been weighed and carefully considered by the elders, for it is only the elders who possess wisdom, knowledge, experience. Only they know and can perceive in everything that invisible part which brings misfortune. Today, alone and isolated, he needed them, he needed their advice. He had never before had to brave alone that formidable adversary, the unknown.

Thierno asked himself what he had come to do in the city with his wife. In his mind, he was transported to his village, to the huts, the families, the clans, the meagre livestock, the fields whose soil had become barren. It was as though he could see the whole of his past life as if frozen, clear and definite before him.

The famine had been a terrible catastrophe, wiping out animals and humans alike. This cruel and bitter reminder of it upset him very much. There was no future that he could see, no hope for any future whatsoever. It was only the present, and the immediate concern of the moment – to go and bury his dead son – which was determining his actions.

The stops went by, one after another. People walked past, brisk, alert, hardly ever speaking to one another. In every movement, every look, smouldered intense activity. Everything was strange to him, these people with their own particular reactions to things. He avoided meeting the eyes of the other passengers, afraid that he would betray himself. At each stop, he was beset by the same fears. The elder, the old ragman, had said to him:

'It's at the stops that you must be careful. In the city, you can never know who your neighbour is ▸.'

After some moments of silence, he had added: 'In the city, you must never trust anyone.'

An intruder burst into his closed universe. Like a surprised animal, on the alert, Thierno regained his self-control and turned to look outside. He wondered who this disturbing presence could be, sitting next to him. A man? A woman? He shrank back even more, holding his breath. A man of the open spaces, who had sometimes been a hunter, he was able to contain himself so as not to alarm the beast.

The passenger settled himself down, quite at ease, pushing against him a little. Thierno moved closer to the window. The other man opened his newspaper expansively. Thierno leaned on his right side, pulling his son's corpse over. His eyes crept slowly up, taking in the well-polished brown ankle-boots, the neat pleats of the trousers. The European clothes were associated for him with the world of chiefs, bosses, well-off people. The proximity of the man irked him, put him on edge. Wary, he kept his distance. His 'neighbour' was an important person.

The neighbour spread out his newspaper aggressively. Its rustling sound made Thierno tremble: it evoked in his religious consciousness that myth of writing as the consecration of all knowledge, which imparts authority to all who possess it. He wedged himself in as well as he could against the metal. A sudden hot flush left him clammy. The bottom of the newspaper was resting on the dead child's feet: a fold of the shroud, in that spot, was coming undone. Was his secret going to be exposed? He could not tear his eyes from the spot. Terror gripped him. He was suffocating. He felt as though he were sharing this feeling of being stifled with Niiwam. His heart beat louder and louder. He drew in his empty stomach even more. The newspaper page, stuck to the cloth, followed the contours of its folds. Was he screaming inside himself? There was no sound echoing outside. He raised his eyes to look at the other man. They were separated by the newspaper, but this partition only added to his alarm. The way his neighbour – who was definitely a boss – was dressed, completely unnerved him. Thierno was struck by the man's large wrist-watch.

The man lowered his paper. Distant, stern, commanding, he stared hard at Thierno over the paper. He was searching, probing. The muscles in Thierno's face started twitching. He felt disturbed, uneasy. A building was reflected in the man's white glasses. Cowed, Thierno turned his eyes back to Niiwam. He wanted to lift the paper from the lifeless body, but he did not have the courage to do so. He humbled himself. Was this an escape? And was it a real or a contrived one?

The man in European clothing calmly resumed his reading, satisfied that he had put him in his place.

The seconds and minutes were going by slowly. The route of the number eight bus stretches out over twenty-six kilometres. Each trip is scheduled to last one and a half hours; at rush hour the schedule allows for two hours. Two teams of two people each were working in shifts; the first from six in the morning until two in the afternoon, the second from two until nine at night.

Wellé, the driver, wanted to make up the ten minutes lost on his second trip. He was teamed up with Malan Cissé, a veteran of the line. This conductor had no patience with passengers who dawdled. Apart from checking the tickets, he ruled over the departures as well as the halts. Malan knew a good number of the regulars on the line. His small sharp eyes missed nothing that went on in the bus. He would declare to anyone who cared to hear it that he had 'a very good visual memory'.

Since they had left, Wellé had been beating all the red lights. What a stroke of luck! It gave him pleasure to hear the engine purring; he enjoyed the technicalities of his job. At this rate, he could be sure of arriving ahead of time, and being able to smoke a cigarette without rushing it. Already he was savouring the smoke in anticipation.

The bus left the Presidential Palace behind, and rumbled along the Boulevard de la République, turning into President Lamine-Gueye Avenue. It was a major thoroughfare, lined with mosques, shops well-stocked with imported fabrics and beauty products, a cinema, restaurants, pharmacies, cobblers' stalls, hairdressers and Asian bazaars. The clientèle frequenting the avenue consisted mainly of women. In front of one of the mosques, traditional embroiderers sat working on sheepskins or mats spread on the pavement.

It was a one-way street until the crossing. Wellé used the brakes, moving forward in fits and starts. He stayed in the second lane, avoiding the row of illegally parked cars and keeping his eye on the rear-view mirror so that he could double park. He got to his bus stop, only to see a Mercedes 600 parked there ... and with a D number plate: Diplomatic Corps.

Someone had rung for this stop. The three doors opened.

The man in the grey terylene suit – Thierno's neighbour – meticulously folded his newspaper, and stood up. Thierno had his back turned to him. The window framed the man's tall, slender silhouette, blurred against a layer of fine dust. Thierno was observing him, on his guard. He was convinced of the man's hostility. Curled up in a ball, he watched him closely.

On the pavement, the man felt in his pockets, and pulled out a massive packet of Marlboros and a gold lighter. He lit a cigarette and walked away elegantly.

Thierno breathed a deep sigh of relief. He stretched his legs and gently pulled Niiwam onto his lap to rearrange the shroud. He kept his ticket in between the folds of the cloth, this thread-bare, yellowed sheet which the hospital had thrown out and which the old ragman had given him. He settled himself comfortably, his watchful eye wandering around inside the bus, and then outside.

A young blind boy was sitting on the ground under a plane tree, shouting out some religious refrain that was making him hoarse. He was begging for food. A woman next to him was selling grilled peanuts and feeding her newborn child huddled on her lap. She rocked her child backwards and forwards, lulling it with her chanting, all the while putting her peanuts into bags.

Thierno thought, with a pang of compassion, of his dead son. He felt sad at the sight of this mother with her baby sitting next to the blind youth.

He emerged from the abyss into which his morbid thoughts had plunged him only when the bus came to an abrupt halt. The red traffic light, like a blazing eye, insistent and authoritative, forced him back to reality. Right near the pole, a policeman in khaki, eyes hidden behind dark glasses and the peak of his cap pulled down to his eyebrows, was directing the traffic.

Both the policeman and the bleeding red point reminded him of the power of authority whose invisible claws held him in their clutch ... crushing him ... Was he guilty? Of what? And why? Was he feeling the weight of the fault he had committed? An offence against whom? The sense that he had violated the norms of the living was growing in him! One does not travel around with a corpse that nobody knows about. He felt lost with Niiwam in a strange land. He regretted ever leaving his village and his community.

Again, his eyes fell on the symbol of power. He tried to hide from the policeman's glasses by sliding down into his seat. (Between you and me, the policeman could see neither him nor his corpse of a son.)

The light changed to green.

Wellé stepped hard on the accelerator. The hundred and sixty horses reared and galloped off, letting loose a thick black cloud of smoke. Wellé had the same habits as any heavy-vehicle driver.

The bus came to the crossroads.

The Sandaga market, in Sahelian Sudanese style, is surrounded by stalls and booths and offers a wide variety of wares: shoes, radios, transistor radios, attaché-cases, cream for making women's dark skins light, bras, women's slips. The same national music station was blaring out at a high rate of decibels from all the transistors. Like ants whose anthill has been crushed by some careless foot, people were swarming around, scurrying from one side of the market to the other. The bright, warm, gaudy, shimmering colours of their clothes tossed the sun's rays between them. Shouts and cries, the clamour of voices and policemen's whistles competed against the transistor radios. The stench of rotten fish, dried fish, meat going off, dead cats and dogs decomposing, filthy, stagnant water, the smell of chilis, pepper, onions, wet paper, of feet festering with incurable sores, and of sweat and engine oil, all mingled together, wafting and hanging heavy in the air.

Wellé, the driver, hated this part of the journey. Pedestrians wandered nonchalantly from pavement to pavement, paying no attention to the cars in the road. Paralytics crawled between the machines like eels in water. He was on his guard, and drove slowly, cautiously. He became more and more frustrated with every precious minute he was losing.

At the 'Union' bus stop, housewives took the bus by storm. Calabashes, plastic buckets and baskets were swung from hand to hand, coming to land finally on laps. Women's voices engaged in conversations which turned almost exclusively on the high cost of living. The smell of foodstuffs and spices tantalised the nostrils.

An old blind man and his guide, both singing, tried to get on at the middle door.

'Come on, off with you,' Malan the conductor shouted at them. His powerful voice drew the passengers' attention to the disabled man and his guide.

'Malan, you don't treat innocent people like that,' a woman who was still standing up shouted at him, balancing her calabash in the palm of her hand. She knew the conductor.

'The pavement is where beggars belong,' Malan replied in an annoyed voice, his face impassive.

The blind man, his mouth still open, held his song unfinished in the back of his throat. In spite of his blindness, his eyelids without lashes were lifted up, opening onto the void. Without hesitating, he clasped the shoulder of the little boy who was his guide, and climbed down, feeling his way with his feet.

Startled by the conductor's stern voice, Thierno had looked around anxiously. Malan scrutinized everybody on the bus before sitting down again.

'Ey, Ndyesan!' murmured the woman who had sat down next to Thierno.

She was gazing at him.

The departure. A few spins of the wheel. Thierno peered into the woman's calabash: bits of white-fleshed cassava made his mouth water. He had not eaten for over twenty-four hours, and the sight of the tubers sharpened his gnawing hunger pangs. He swallowed his saliva, and looked outside. At every stop, his neighbour's thighs would crash against the corpse's feet.

Thierno wondered if his wife had gone home. But how? It was he, the man, who had refused to let her come with him. His religion forbade women to attend burials. He had forgotten that without a single centime his wife could not go anywhere. And now another woman was sitting next to him. Thinking of this was getting him nowhere.

Instinctively, his eyes started wandering around the bus again. He was relieved, all the passengers had their backs to him, and he had nothing in front of him but necks. He marvelled every time the little red light saying 'arrêt demandé*, lit up. He couldn't read French. His elder, the old ragman, had forgotten to tell him about that. Distracted by this red light which kept flashing on and off, he started to relax. His face took on its usual peaceful expression. He leaned his head back, and looked up. The sky was flowing past ...

'Excuse me ... Excuse me, mister.'

The woman had startled him out of his rêverie. He stared at her. She stood up, her calabash still balanced on her right palm. The housewife had noticed the man's shining eyes. She batted

* Translator's note: 'Stop requested'

her eyelashes coyly, and made her way nonchalantly to the door. Thierno, as a result of his upbringing, hated forwardness in women, especially young women. Nevertheless, as his mind was wandering, his eyes, fascinated, never left the woman's backside.

On the other side of the window, a vendor selling fritters came up to present his wares: big greasy fritters, full of oil. The vendor lifted the tray right up to him. Thierno was desperate. He stared at the food, panting as thought he had just run a long race. The spasms in his stomach grew stronger. He suddenly felt dizzy; tiny drops of perspiration glistened on his forehead and neck. He had a lump in his throat and his mouth was filled with saliva, yet he refused to ask. His self-respect made it impossible for him to beg.

The vendor could see that this man was hungry. He moved along to the middle door which was still open, and twirled his tray around on the tips of his fingers, watching Thierno all the time, and calling out:

'They're good and warm
They taste good
They're soft
They're sweet
If your teeth break when you bite
This sugared cake
It's because your tooth was loose
They're good and warm.'

Malan rang the bell announcing their departure ... The vendor was disappointed by this poor wretch, and as he retreated, glared scornfully at Thierno.

The bus doors closed again.

● ● ●

At the Tilleen market, a cloud of pervasive blue flies settled on the sheet covering Niiwam. In small, tenacious clumps, they circled around the blood stains.

Thierno delicately waved them away. Some of them flew from face to face or from neck to neck; some were crawling on the chrome bars, others on the edges of the windows and on the hanging straps, and then returning to the charge again. Every movement Thierno made seemed only to attract more of them. He felt frightened, a vague sort of fear which made him forget his hunger. He peered hurriedly at the people as he tried to protect Niiwam from the onslaught of the flies. He hugged the body affectionately, covering it with his forearm. Suddenly, he lifted his arms: their weight on the body filled him with remorse. That was sacrilege! Gently, he ran his hands over the lifeless form, and rocked Niiwam slowly backwards and forwards to keep the flies away.

Had he been such a caring father when the child was still alive? Had he shown his son this much tenderness while he lived? Was not his only concern to feed him? He used to leave early in the morning and come back late at night to place before his wife the day's meagre gains, obtained at so high a price. When the child showed the first symptoms, his wife had taken care of him. She had turned first to old wives' remedies. Then came the healers and marabouts. And when in spite of all this there was still no improvement, the mother had gone to the only clinic in Guedjway. The child had to be hospitalised. He was to be moved to the 'Native Hospital'. He was admitted to the paediatric ward: 'Housewives' Ward'. The mother and infant were fortunate: they found a mat and slept on the cold cement. Without proper care, the baby had lasted only that night, its last. The next day, he breathed his last.

In the morning, Thierno had experienced no difficulty – no administrative difficulty – in obtaining the burial permit and the death certificate, the reason being that the only cold room was filled with the bodies of important people. Sometimes they do not preserve the bodies of the poor.

This was the second child he had lost. The first had been

buried in the village without any administrative problem and without the need for public transport. The community had taken care of everything.

Thierno, shaped by the experiences he had lived through, had become a fatalist, blaming whatever happened on fate. He was motivated by a spiritual force which grew out of his faith, and which demanded that he bury his son's corpse in a cemetery reserved for Muslims. He clung to this idea without ever asking himself if it would be possible. For today, this was the single aim of his life, of his existence. Tomorrow would be another day. He remembered the kindness of the attendant at the morgue, of the warden and the old ragman. He was not without regrets: he had not learned their names. He felt guilty about this negligence. He resolved to return, once he had buried his son, to excuse himself for his carelessness towards them.

By now Wellé was free of the heavy traffic in Blaise-Diagne Avenue and the Tilleen market, and had got up a good speed. From Ouakam Road he forked off to the right before the entrance to the university, and headed towards Stage E. At the intersection, a group of onlookers was blocking the way: a brand new yellow Chrysler had collided with a white Renault. There were red marks on the asphalt, and two road-safety officers were busy on the scene. Wellé manoeuvred a way through by driving with his left wheels on the pavement, while Malan helped by keeping an eye on the back of the bus.

The slanting right side of the bus drew level with the accident. Thierno could not tear his eyes from the large pool of coagulating blood. Just then one of the wheels bumped hard against the curb, and Niiwam's head was banged against the metal panel. Thierno jumped, his eyes wild. He had felt the shock going through his own bones. He remained half-upright on his knees until the driver's manoeuvres were over.

The flies had disappeared as if by magic.

At the next stop, schoolchildren from Blaise-Diagne took the bus by storm. They spoke Franwolof * in loud, shrill voices. They held out their tickets, each one in turn displaying a season ticket.

One of the passengers had attracted Malan's attention: a young man wearing a very clean white shirt, tailored in the waist, and tight trousers with no back pockets. He had a smooth, youthful face, a fashionable, bushy hairstyle, and almond-shaped eyes that darted about inquisitively. Standing in front of the conductor, he undid his right sleeve and took out a rolled-up note. Malan, thinking he was going to be talked out of a fare, felt immediately hostile. The young man, relaxed, was joking around, and flashed him a compelling smile. His eyes narrowed. He oozed polite charm. He unfolded the five hundred franc note, smoothed it out reverently before giving it to the conductor, and said in French:

'Airport terminus!'

Malan dug around in his memory trying to remember this young man. He was sure that he had seen him before. But where? And in what context? Malan had to collect the other passengers' tickets, and so could not recall exactly the circumstances of the encounter. After he had given him his change, he watched him and saw him speaking to another passenger who had got on at the previous stop. The latter, who wore a spotless white caftan, was carrying a grey briefcase. Malan could not hear what they were saying. The two separated, and sat in different rows. He racked his brains. He was intrigued by these two young men.

The bus started up Dial-Diop Boulevard, and then took Bourguiba Avenue, hurtling down the gentle slope to the by-pass onto the Puits road. It passed the Xar Yalla police barracks and was swallowed up in the Grand-Yoff district.

The scenery was suburban: another densely populated area of Dakar. Women, together with dirty sheep and naked or half-naked urchins with bloated bellies and scrawny legs were congregated around the public taps; people were selling water,

* Translator's note: patois, a mixture of French and Wolof.

and carts, ducks, chickens and dogs wandered about.

Wellé gripped the steering wheel firmly and settled himself squarely in his seat. He checked his two rear-view mirrors constantly. It needed only the slightest incident, and he and his colleague would be in trouble. It said in the instructions they had received that they were to be careful as they came into this zone.

Wellé, checking again in his left rear-view mirror, saw a fast mini-bus bearing down on him, racing to get to the waiting clients first. Wellé did not like the drivers of those mini-buses. They clung so dogmatically to the principle of 'first come, first served'. He swung the steering-wheel to the left, and brought his bus into the middle of the road, forcing the other one to follow him and swallow his plume of smoke. He was impervious to its repeated hooting.

Malan kept watch behind. He shared his thoughts at the top of his voice:

'His chin is scraping the ground, the dog! An eyesore on wheels, that's what he's driving! To the scrapheap, you prick! Hee! Hee! Hee!'

The driver of the minibus was cursing, making vulgar gestures which accompanied his inaudible words. Wellé accelerated and put a good distance between them. He had planned his move well: there were no sheep or children now to get in the way. Satisfied by his own expertise, he pulled the right side of the bus over onto the side of the road. The doors slid open. Pleased with himself, Wellé leaned back in his seat, a victorious smile playing over his fat face.

The minibus driver drew level with Wellé. He slowed down to treat him to a fine sample of obscene language, which was greeted with bursts of laughter from the passengers. Relieved, he continued on his way.

Thierno was incensed by the driver's foul language.

'*Assalaa-Maleykum*,' came a man's voice.

'*Maleykum-Salam*,' chorused the people in the bus.

Thierno was charmed by the quality of the voice and turned around to see who had arrived. The man was well on in years, but held himself erect. A goatee adorned his chin. He was dressed all in white, with a skullcap on his freshly shaven head. He had on his shoulder a white turban, from Mecca, and in his right hand a rosary of ebony beads and carved silver. He had a Koran and a carpet clasped under his right arm. A lingering smell of musk emanated from his whole person. He went before each passenger, men and women alike, emphasising his '*Alham doullilah's*' by the way he nodded his head. As he came up next to Thierno, he repeated his refrain. Thierno could not stop looking at him. He was captivated.

The marabout gathered up the folds of his large boubou and sat down on the side bench, his every movement accompanied by the endless '*Bissimilah*'. When he was comfortably seated, he started up a formal conversation with Wellé.

Thierno would have loved to have him sit next to him. 'A saintly man! A great marabout!' he said to himself.

As for Malan, he never once took his eyes off the young man. He was struggling to place him. Twice their eyes had met. The conductor was convinced that he had had something to do with this young man before. Where? And when? The passengers streamed past in front of him ...

Thierno felt ill at ease when a woman came and sat down next to him, on his left. He pressed himself into the corner and pulled his legs up under him, squeezing his thighs. He shifted Niiwam to his right, avoiding all contact with the woman. She was well dressed, in African style, wearing an afro wig, her eyes hidden behind a large pair of dark glasses. A younger woman, in horse-riding clothes – blue jeans, a shirt with a fringe falling to her buttocks, and a sling bag which she was constantly hoisting back onto her shoulder – was with her.

'Let's hope we'll get there on time,' said the younger woman, sitting down in front.

She noticed Thierno. Suddenly she looked disdainful. She

pulled a face, and nudged her companion. The pair of glasses
focused on Thierno. He knew that he was being watched, and
set his jaw. He felt alienated by the two young women's rude-
ness.

'Weasels,' he thought contemptuously.

He put his left hand in between Niiwam and the woman, so
that nothing should sully his dead son. Then he chased away
the flies which had returned. His neighbour sent them back with
an airy wave of her hand, making a scornful sound between her
teeth. He was fuming at his helplessness against the flies and
against the woman.

He looked outside, his mind wandering … free.

The bus had started on its journey again. Little kids were
having fun running across the road in front of the vehicle. They
jumped up, now on the left, now on the right. Wellé's patience
was being tried. He had to restrain himself from exploding with
rage, and cursing all mothers and fathers. He slowed down to
let them cross.

Thierno thought these children were reckless. As he watched
them, he thought of the lifeless form on his lap, and felt a rush
of tenderness for his dead child. His emotion swelled. He
sniffed, and this attracted the woman's attention. From the
corner of his eye, Thierno watched for her reaction.

Lamenting the fact that he had let himself go in the presence
of another person, he choked back his grief. Because of his pride,
he was able to assume a brave front. He looked over at the
marabout and noticed that his large ears were sticking out.

The travellers were being jolted and thrown about. Thierno's
shoulder bumped against his neighbour. The corpse's joined
feet hit the woman in the stomach. She roughly pushed Thierno
away. He started, his face tense and angry. Rust-coloured eyes
darting fire moved rapidly from one woman to the other.

The other one, the horse-rider, stared back at him, unflinching.

The bus's wheels came out of the pot-holes. The passengers
settled down again. Wellé allowed a funeral procession at the

entrance to the Patte-d'Oie to go ahead of him.

'It's the funeral of one of the country's great sons,' one man said.

'May Allah, in his infinite goodness, assist him,' pronounced the marabout.

'*Amine! Amine! Amine!*' came the echo of voices.

'A very important man,' added someone who was reciting some verses of the Koran under his breath.

'More than twenty cars? What a convoy! I've never seen so many people.'

Thierno heard these comments. Holding Niiwam tight, he had sat up so that he could see too. The hearse, without wreaths or flowers, rolled by slowly, trailing behind it a line of cars of every European make.

• • •

When Wellé came out of the Patte-d'Oie and turned onto the road to Yoff, he had lost quite a few minutes from his schedule. He hoped to make up at least some of the time, and looked at his watch: the second-hand was ticking around jerkily. He badly needed to urinate; he had been feeling twinges ever since the Tilleen section. His weak bladder had always been a handicap. He didn't dare to stop to relieve himself. If the inspector caught him, he stood a good chance of being fired … especially as the city was teeming with drivers looking for work.

There was a burst of laughter, a sound as strange as a clap of thunder in the dry season. It aroused the passengers' curiosity, and they turned around to see what the cause of this merriment was, and who was responsible for it. The marabout pointed with his chin. He begged Yallah for pity and forgiveness for having witnessed this shamelessness. Thierno had shuddered. Uneasy as he was, he thought he had been found out. Deep in his eyes the shadow of fear was lurking. He eyed the two women, who both lowered their eyes. Malan rang the bell twice, asking for a stop. Wellé braked. The doors opened and an old woman struggled up, panting.

'Malan, I thank you,' she gasped, out of breath. Then to the driver: 'Wellé, may Yallah reward you for your goodness. I greet you, fellow travellers.'

Everyone returned her greeting.

All those who worked on line eight knew Ma M'Bengue. She sat down at the other side bench, facing the marabout, and exchanged some words with him. The marabout was well-known for his weekly visits to the cemetery, every Friday. He never shook hands with a woman. He turned to face in front of him, to avoid looking at the old woman.

The bus pulled off. Thierno, feeling confused, looked carefully at the scenery. The old ragman had given him detailed descriptions of the places he would be passing through.

On his right the shacks of the Grand-Medina* were flowing past. Perched on the hill overlooking the plain, shrivelled baobabs, bare in that season, arrested the eye with their fantastic forms in the vast expanses. Women and little girls were walking in single file over the dune, carrying the containers they had taken to fill at the taps. A clump of mango trees rose half hidden from between two mounds of sand. Electric wires dotted with red and black balls ran along the side of the road. Further on loomed the oval shape of the new Friendship Stadium.

On the left, above the embankment of the road, appeared the cone-shaped roofs of the warehouses at the Fair, the rows of trees between the buildings, the fence of cement slats, the smooth round stones.

Ahead was the fly-over, its two arches outlined against the sky. In the distance the Layen district and the island of Yoff, naked and curved like the shell of a giant tortoise, were basking in the bright sunlight. Vultures were wheeling in the sky. The sea bristled as the wind breathed gently over it, the fine spray licking over the sea and carrying its iodine smell far away.

* Translator's note: a densely-populated suburb of Dakar.

The bus passed under the fly-over.

Thierno wanted to find out where he was. He turned to look at the woman sitting next to him. She was talking to her friend. The sunglasses made any communication with her impossible for him. He looked at the conductor in his booth: Malan was busy with his accounts, and seemed engrossed. His eyes settled again on the marabout. He stared at the back of the old man's neck, hoping he would turn around. He would have confided in him: a brother in the faith. He did not dare move, for fear of arousing curiosity.

Whom could he approach? Whom could he ask where to find the cemetery? He looked all around as far as he could, but no burial mounds or graves could be seen. He looked at his corpse again. Bunches of flies were collecting on the shroud. A ray of sunlight filtering through the window made a mark on the sheet the size of a fist: two flies were mating there. Thierno was annoyed and chased them off by twitching his wrist. One of them went and sat on the lady's nose, only to be immediately shooed away. The sunglasses, beneath a frowning brow, turned to stare at him.

Thierno looked to his left. Ma M'Bengue was engaged in a friendly discussion with a young man. Her plump wrist fluttered about as though separate from her body, in time to the flow of her words. In the light, her skin seemed to be the colour of clove. Thierno watched his neighbour closely: the earring – a golden pendant; the chrome stem of the frame of her glasses stuck into her wig. The daylight seemed to have sculpted her profile out of reddish wood.

With great caution, Thierno asked: 'Lady, is it the village of Yoff we're coming to?'

He repeated his question in a louder voice.

'Ahan! In front of you.'

'And the stop for the cemetery?'

She spluttered, unable to complete her sentence. With her mouth open, she was staring wide-eyed at the little bundle on the man's lap. She let out a blood-curdling howl, a cry was wrenched from the deepest part of herself. With one swift movement, she gathered the folds of her big boubou around her hips so as to avoid all contact with the parcel.

'There's a corpse on the bus,' she screamed with loathing.

Screams and cries, born of that ancient fear of death, burst out. The air was thick with anguish and phobia. The passengers all got up and rushed for the closed exits. Pandemonium! Everyone was trying to escape ... to get far away from here. They were all pushing and shoving in the narrow aisle. Head-dresses and handkerchiefs were falling to the ground. Thierno's neighbour lost her glasses, which rolled onto the floor. She herself trampled on them without even seeing them. Her equestrian friend was letting out stifled squeals.

Wellé slammed on brakes.

The hysterical passengers crashed into each other. The shouts and cries became even louder.

Thierno was unmoved by all this commotion. He kept calm, but his heart was beating fast, very loud.

'Where is the corpse?' one man asked, holding back his terror.

'There! There!' the hysterical woman shrieked.

Ma M'Bengue came up, pushing everybody out of the way.

'Let me through! Where is this dead person?'

'Here!... Here!...'

People surged back towards Thierno, denouncing him, yet curious. Now everybody wanted to see the 'dead body'. Gradually their vociferations died down.

'Bloody fool! Bastard!' Malan was muttering in French.

He could see only Thierno's back and neck. He was standing in his booth, his head craning over the top bar.

'Eh, you! Don't you know the difference between a bus and a hearse?' he bellowed.

'What is this lunatic doing, Malan? Get him off,' Wellé was shouting. 'And anyway, has he paid?' he added, furious.

His need to urinate was becoming more and more urgent.

The middle door opened, and the smell of the sea flooded into the bus.

'Eh! Have you paid?' Malan asked, his fingers hooked into the wire mesh of his booth.

How had he not seen this corpse? His memory was really playing tricks on him today. He hadn't even been able to place that young man with the five hundred franc note. And yet that guy still reminded him of someone.

At that moment, the young man in question was taking advantage of the commotion to work his way closer to the Amazon, who was standing behind Ma M'Bengue. Keeping an eye on the faces around him, he used his feet, knees and hands to force a way through the people towards her handbag, at the same time joining in the conversation.

'Where's your ticket, old man?' he asked, his face thrust forward.

Thierno was taking note of everything going on around him. His sluggish mind was struggling to draw the link between what he was hearing and himself. He was not in this situation because he had wanted to put on an act of bravado. He had too much respect for other people to be a cynic. He was, without knowing it, humbly obstinate. He carefully took his ticket from between the folds of the shroud and held it up with a trembling hand.

'Ey, Ndyesan! The poor fool! He's a stranger. Do you speak Wolof?' Ma M'Bengue asked him. Her eyes filled with compassion.

Thierno was still seated. He nodded his head, and hugged Niiwam closely. His thoughts were confused, jumbled, out of control. He was alone ... too much alone amongst all these people.

Tongues loosened. Hostility had turned to pity, indulgence. The marabout, a great one for speeches, had launched into a long prophetic exhortation, prophesying the imminent end of the world.

'Malan,' Wellé shouted out again, 'get this guy off. We've lost too much time already.'

He could no longer contain himself, and got up from his seat.

The marabout thought he was going to throw Thierno off the bus, and wanted to intervene. Raising himself up to his full stature, he stretched out his long arms, holding his Koran and his rosary.

But there was something else Wellé had to see to, and with frantic fingers was undoing his fly. Standing next to the front right wheel, he was thoroughly enjoying relieving himself, feeling happy and much lighter. The sound of the stream of urine carried all the way into the bus. Looking into the distance towards the airport runway, he watched the Concorde's graceful take-off, marvelling at its line, fascinated by its technology.

The marabout was still in the same position, when he saw Wellé returning to his place. As it flashed past his vision, he noticed a defiling drop of urine on the man's trousers, a sign of the impurity he loathed in man. His fanatical gaze swept over the gathering. He demanded:

'Wellé, Malan, drive us to the cemetery gate. Let us not forget that Allah is watching over each one of us. Down here we are but ephemeral beings.'

The others approved of the marabout's proposal. They begged the driver to take them there. Ma M'Bengue undid her top loincloth, made of hand-woven cloth, folded it and spread it over the boy Niiwam, carefully chasing away the flies.

Thierno looked up at Ma M'Bengue, whom he did not know. He was deeply moved by such generosity. Losing all restraint, he let his tears flow.

'Don't cry! A man should never cry in front of women,' she consoled him.

Thierno gulped back his tears, his head bowed.

'Ey, Ndyesan,' the young woman with the broken glasses kept saying over and over.

'You're all crazy,' cried Wellé, his hands on the wheel. 'I've got my route and I'm not allowed to go off it. Malan, you are responsible for the vehicle.'

'Hey you ..., get off fast, and take your corpse with you.'

'We haven't got to the board yet. The regulation stop is over there. There's still nearly a hundred metres left to go,' a fellow in a khaki shirt pointed out. He continued in Wolof: 'He's paid to go as far as the stop.'

'I'm telling you ... You heard what I said,' bellowed Malan. 'Speaking about rules, show me your ticket? Naturally, you haven't paid. I'm taking you to the police ... And you ... you get off or I'll tell the driver to take us to the police ...'

He had no sooner said this, than Malan pressed a button, and the doors closed.

'Have a heart, Malan! Be your kind self. The cemetery isn't that far. You ...'

'Ma M'Bengue, you keep quiet ...'

The old woman stopped talking.

'Don't you know that women do not accompany the dead? Are you Muslims or not?' shouted Malan.

Then he addressed Thierno again, speaking more calmly this time:

'Mister, get down. You can see the road ... there ... it's at the end. If the passengers want to go with you, they can.'

'That's right! You are right! Women do not follow funeral processions,' repeated the marabout, who had established himself as spokesman of the faith.

He stared at the horsewoman, disapproving of her immodest attire. He continued volubly: 'Men of the faith must help their brothers in the same religion, who are being tried by sorrow. Stand up, brother in faith! Every child is a chosen one of Allah on this holy Friday. He answers the call of the Lord of us all, down here. '*Allah Akbar*,' he proclaimed in a chanting tone. 'Men, let us fulfil this sacred duty! Let us pay homage to our master.'

With one movement of his arm, he pushed the people back.

The young man – the one who had perplexed the conductor – taking advantage of the marabout's harangue, had during the sermon spirited away the equestrian's purse and slipped it to his accomplice in the caftan. The latter, exploiting the general confusion occasioned by the holy man, led the way, saying loudly and insistently: 'Let him get off ...'

Malan opened the doors again.

Thierno had accepted the marabout's authority. This absolute trust calmed him. He looked at each person in turn. Modestly, humbly, he slowly stood up. The cramps in his stomach made him dizzy, his legs wobbled, but he went determinedly down the aisle. His son's body possessed that dignity which death confers. As he was climbing down he tripped, swayed and stumbled sideways and backwards, but without letting go of Niiwam he regained his balance and narrowed his eyes against the intense heat which made everything seem slightly hazy. He had an excruciating headache.

The passengers who had stayed on the bus had gathered around the doors and windows, crying.

Thierno wobbled with every step that he took, as though he had no will of his own. The pickpocket's accomplice took the corpse from his arms and passed it to the marabout. The latter was inspired and, at the top of his lungs, cried out the lament of the martyrs. The dusty plain of Yoff rang with his song. The thief's accomplice slowed down, detached himself from them and headed in the opposite direction.

The doors of the bus slid closed. Malan gave the order for departure, and the passengers slowly returned to their seats. Ma M'Bengue started reciting in a low voice the prayers for this dead person and for all the dead. The men who stayed behind talked of urgent, important business which made it impossible for them to take part in the convoy. The two women, recovered from all their emotional upheavals, sat down side by side. The Amazon, before she sat down, noticed that her handbag was wide open. She plunged her hand into it: her purse with more than a hundred thousand francs inside it had disappeared. She screamed:

'Stop! Stop! I've been robbed!'

She stamped her feet. She got down and crawled on the ground, feeling around for her purse. Her friend helped her, picking up the pieces of her broken glasses. The two of them searched amongst feet and baskets, in vain. They couldn't find it, and stood up again.

'Driver, stop … Stop! Someone has stolen all my money!' shrieked the horsewoman.

The others watched them, unconcerned.

By now Wellé was really fed up. In a while he would have to explain why he was so late. He was waiting for the order to stop the bus, but Malan had turned a deaf ear to the woman's screams. His eyes were fixed on the young man's neck. His memory had returned: this young man was a pickpocket. He glanced out of the back window. In the distance the accomplice, his white caftan standing out clearly against the cream-coloured ground, was walking off with a light step.

The line of cars of the other funeral, now driving ahead of the hearse, was heading back up to the main road.

The marabout and Thierno kept vanishing into the hollows between the dunes and then reappearing. Thierno had taken Niiwam again, and was holding him in his arms. The wind wiped all trace of their steps from the sand, as it carried away the echo of the lament of the martyrs.

Taaw

THE *'ASSALÂÂÂ-MALEÏKUM'*, UTTERED in a chanting voice, marked the end of the prayer of Fadjar – the first prayer of the new day. The sea breeze, heavy with iodine, came in from the coast and carried the echo over tin roofs, tiled roofs, flat roofs, all still steeped in lingering darkness.

In the sky, a few stars began to pale.

Inside the wooden mosque, three lightbulbs shed a yellowish light. The darkness of the outer shadows formed a circle around this empty space of light; on mats and sheepskins a congregation of a dozen or so, lined up in a row and a half behind the Imam, were telling their beads. The monastic silence was broken only by the 'tick, tick' of the clock which hung to the right above the Imam's recess, and by the regular click of beads.

In the distance a vague murmur could be heard, like that of the sea just before the turning of the tide.

The shopkeeper stood in the middle doorway, bare-chested and wearing nothing but a loincloth. He held his arms above his head, locked his fingers together and, on tiptoe, stretched deliciously, yawning. He looked up at the sky, then turned his gaze to the road. Five women, empty basins under their arms, were making their way to the well.

Every morning of his *mômé*[1] with his first wife Yaye[2] Dabo, Baye Tine took the same route and walked past the same men and women. Since his retirement seven years before, he had been taking the road to the mosque instead of his former path to the woodworks. Of average build, but rather short, Baye Tine

Author's note: [1] the number of days that a polygamist spends with one of his wives. The same term refers to the wife who receives her husband. Translator's note: [2] Mother wore two or three boubous and kept his breast-pocket padded with a thick wallet. He was rotund and sported a prominent pot-belly. With his red cap tilted to one side and old Moroccan slippers for shoes, he walked with his feet turned out, dragging his heels.

Back at the concession he shared with several other families, he settled himself in the yard near his shack, facing the east to finish telling his beads.

Rays of light filtered through the cracks between the poorly fitted boards around the doors and windows. Children were shaken out of sleep by whispering, murmuring, sharp admonitions.

Uncertain at first, dawn eventually brightened the east.

'*Assalamaleïkum*, Tine.' Amady the cart-driver called out his greeting as he did every morning, going off with his kettle to wet his horse's hooves.

'Amady, you are a practising Muslim and believer. Why do you insist on performing this pagan ritual every morning before you've even said your prayers?' Baye Tine asked him.

'Baye Tine, I am a believer at heart: you can bear witness to that on the day I die. But I have to see to my livelihood. Wetting my horse's hooves drives away the evil eye and the forked tongues,' Amady answered when he had finished his rite.

Once alone, Baye Tine started his Fadjar prayer. He was well-read in Arabic, and recited the Sura[1] in a pleasingly resonant voice. His arafes[2] too, were always perfectly pronounced.

Baye Tine reverently thanked Yallah for the gift of this new day. He prayed fervently for divine grace, first for his own family, and then for all Muslims on earth. Palms pressed together, he held between his two thumbs a rosary which he rubbed over his face before standing up. Then he went over to the door of the lean-to where his sons were sleeping, and pushed it open.

Translator's note: [1] chapter of the Koran; [2] letters of the Arabic alphabet.

There was a burst of shrill cries.

'Father! Father, I'm sorry ... Father, forgive me!' cried a child's hollow voice over and over.

Abdou, naked, clutched his father's wrist with both hands and walked behind him on tip-toe: Baye Tine was pinching the child's ear, forcing him up. He settled himself on the floor and laid his son down, gripping his head under his right knee and twisting the boy's arm. He dug up the stick he had buried the night before and began to beat Abdou's buttocks.

'Where were you yesterday?' his father demanded.

The child's screams put paid to the last moments of sleep of the other inhabitants of the concession. The grown-ups were used to these morning thrashings and began to go about their affairs, ignoring Abdou's cries for help.

'I, your father, register you at Daraa, the Koranic school, and you – you half-wit, good-for-nothing, you play truant!'

The stick beat down on naked flesh. Abdou squirmed and writhed, shrieking fit to wake the dead. As he beat him, Baye Tine shouted: 'You think you're a man now? You little brat! I'll skin you alive before I see you turn into a hooligan or a crook.'

'Father, forgive me! Mother! Mother ... come and help me! Taaw! Taaw! Father, I'm going to die ... I have to urinate ... Father, I won't bunk the Daraa again ...'

'You little liar! This is the tenth time you've told me the same thing,' replied Baye Tine, impervious to his son's pleading.

Yaye Dabo, his mother, came rushing out of the room, tying her loincloth firmly, her blouse inside out.

'He's learnt his lesson by now,' she said to her husband, holding back the hand clutching the stick.

'Look here!... Just look at this ... the dog has wet me!' exclaimed Baye Tine, pushing Abdou away roughly.

The child lay stretched out at his father's feet. Then, on all fours, he crawled over to his mother and clung to her legs.

'The little devil has soiled my pants,' complained the father. 'You dare refuse to learn the Koran, and I'll slit your throat,' he added, standing up and facing his wife.

Together they examined the mark on his trousers. 'He's only a child, he's still pure. I'll go and rinse it,' Yaye Dabo said soothingly.

She had spoken instinctively, out of obedience, rather than from the desire to reply, stifling the surges of revolt she felt rising inside her.

'And as for that one there! ... Just look at him ...'

Baye Tine called his neighbours' attention with a sweep of his hand.

'He's waiting for a job to fall from the sky. It's him, it's all his fault, he's the one who influences the children. He sets them a very bad example.'

Baye Tine was referring to his oldest son Taaw, who was just stepping out of the little room, wearing loose cotton khaki pants, with a filthy black-and-green-striped towel flung over his shoulder. Baye Tine moved aggressively towards him, speaking in a loud, harsh voice.

'Instead of looking for a job, he just lounges around all day. Good for nothing son!'

Yaye Dabo held back her fear. Taaw, a spindly boy with protruding ribs, had a pot of water in his hand; he set about his morning ablutions, washing his face and brushing his teeth with his forefinger.

'*Tchim*!' the father taunted his son. And then he added accusingly to his wife: 'Did you know that he had gone and got Goor Yummbul's daughter pregnant?'

'Taaw, don't answer him,' Yaye Dabo silently pleaded.

Amady the cart-driver, harnesses hooked over his arm, whispered to his neighbour Sy, who was setting off with his two little boys for school: 'Baye Tine's blood has gone bad. He spent the night with his anger.'

'Sons must obey their fathers,' Mr Sy rejoined distantly.

He gave the cart-driver a cold stare, and then added for the benefit of his sons: 'You see what happens when you disobey? Come on then, on we go.'

Mr Sy, who was an orderly at the new town hall and wore khaki, worked hard at being different from other people. Amady watched him going off and said to himself: 'The old fossil thinks of himself as a government official. Doesn't he know that I've been lending his wife money? Poverty hardens our hearts.'

In the meantime, Taaw finished washing, taking absolutely no notice of his father's abuse. Now they found themselves face to face.

Glowering, his eyes dark with suppressed anger, Taaw stared straight at his father. Baye Tine was enraged by his son's scornful looks. His blood was boiling. He pushed Taaw roughly aside, crying, 'Hit me again. You're good at that ... Hit me! You've already broken one of my teeth ... Why don't you knock the rest out too!'

Yaye Dabo, deeply distressed by this scene, looked around, beseeching help. Her eyes met her son's. She shook her head, as if to say: 'Don't answer back!'

Just two years before, Taaw had come to blows with his father and had broken two of his teeth. Arriving home from the late-night movie, he had found his father beating his mother again. Yaye Dabo was screaming herself hoarse, crying for help. As soon as they saw Taaw, both his younger brothers, in tears, clung onto him. Taaw broke down the door.

Inside the candlelit room, Baye Tine was beating Yaye Dabo with his strap, pinning her to the ground with one foot on her back. Taaw grabbed his father and punched him a number of times before dealing him a striking blow to the head. Baye Tine collapsed and fainted.

The neighbours all came running. During the night, the rumour spread that Taaw had killed his father. The next day, Baye Tine laid charges of assault against his son. Arrested and tried, Taaw was given a six-month prison sentence. His mother's account was not considered. 'No matter what the reason might be, a son does not have the right to hit his father,' had been the pronouncement of the old men come to support Baye Tine.

An example was needed.

On his release, Taaw had returned home, for his mother's sake. Yaye Dabo made him swear never again to lift a finger against his father, even if he were about to cut her throat.

Ever since this altercation, father and son had not spoken to each other.

'Hit me again!' bellowed Baye Tine, thrusting his face forward. 'Cursed boy, I'll never forgive you for what you did. Ungrateful son!'

Taaw, silent, clenching his teeth, struggled with his feelings of rebellion. His whole body expressed contempt, and the shadow of a scornful smile played about his lips.

'Go on, break all my teeth,' clamoured Baye Tine, opening his mouth.

Yaye Dabo was deeply distressed, but kept quiet. The resentment which had built up in her during their quarrels and the beatings she had received gave her enough strength to remain outwardly calm. She hated all men, except her father and her sons. She gently slid her hand over Abdou's back, to try and soothe him. The child huddled against her thighs.

'Calm down, Baye Tine,' Amady the cart-driver intervened, placing himself between the two.

Quick-tempered, Baye Tine lashed out with a torrent of abuse.

'One should not wish so much harm on one's own son.'

'I hope he'll be the laughing-stock of all his friends. I fed and raised him. And you, Amady, have you any idea how the son of a dog thanks me?'

Taaw took advantage of the carter's presence to slip away to the little room. Baye Tine continued his litany of insult and abuse.

Yaye Dabo gave thanks to Yallah.

'Mother, I'm going out,' called Taaw. He was wearing an anango* outfit of pale green cloth printed with red flowers, and

---

* Translator's note: long and wide-sleeved dress worn by men. Borrowed from the Nago-Nango, a local ethnic group.

old Adidas tackies on his feet.

'Go in peace,' answered his mother.

'Son of a dog! Bastard! And don't you come back to this house either,' Baye Tine shouted after him.

A large, creamy-white cloth was pulled across the sky, restoring to objects their shapes and colours: trees, houses, fences and television aerials took on their distinct forms. Voices and other sounds reverberated clearly.

That morning, Taaw again fled the house. He nursed a persistent hatred for his father, and the loathing that he felt all the time would reach breaking-point whenever his father either beat his brother or abused his mother. His pride was wounded by his mother's humiliation. He believed that his father had sacrificed them for the pleasure he enjoyed with his second wife.

Instinctively, Taaw headed for the 'place of the jobless', as the young people of the area had come to call their meeting-ground. To his great surprise, he found two of the Mbengues there: the Joker, dressed as always in his leopard outfit, with a knitted beret in the national colours perched on his dreadlocks, and Mam Ass, scrawny in his patched and pocketless jeans, a pearl necklace around his neck, and his woollen hat, worn Cabral style, on his head.

'Hey! Boy! What's this? You fell out of bed or something?' exclaimed Taaw, surprised and delighted at having company so early in the morning.

'No! ... No! ... Boy. We fell off the mat,' Mam Ass jokingly replied.

He took two quick drags on his cigarette and handed it to Mbengue. Mbengue inhaled deeply and passed it to Taaw. 'It's too early, I've got an empty stomach. The old man woke me up, he was hitting the kid again.'

'That's too much, boy! All these old fossils can do is throw their weight around – just the day before yesterday, my old man beat up Number Two so badly that she's still out of action. The old bag was bleating like a goat ... Baa! Baa! Baa!' Mbengue went on in imitation.

'Boy, don't you want a hit? It makes you sharp first thing in the morning,' Mam Ass persisted.

Taaw pushed away the cigarette rolled up in old newspaper. He drew his head back, avoiding the thin wisp of curling smoke.

'No thanks, boy! I already told you I've got an empty stomach. And fathers? They're too much, I tell you … All they can do is carry on and on: "In my time this, in my time that. You must find a job." And as soon as they've got some bucks, they go off and find themselves a new chick. And they call us lazy.'

'Hey boy, you should do what I do. As soon as the dinosaur starts up his old record again, I just tune into reggae in my head.'

'These old folk are really out of touch,' was Mbengue's conclusion.

'Boy, why don't you come with me to the Labour Office.'

Mbengue stared at Taaw.

'Hey, boy, you cracked or something? You better watch out for your old lady, she's witchdoctored you. The only thing you can say is "work", "work". Open your eyes, boy … Work never made anyone richer. Look at our fathers …'

'It's true, boy, Mbengue's right,' Mam Ass added, interrupting Mbengue.

'Why drive yourself to the end of the earth? And come back with dust? I'm going to fart, guys.'

Mbengue lifted his leg to let off a loud fart.

'Boy, you're still alive and already rotten inside! What have you been eating?'

Taaw took a few steps backwards. Mam Ass got up from the bench holding his nose.

'So what? I stuffed myself with beans.'

Mbengue was fond of this slang, a mixture of Wolof, French and English. With no respect for age or place, he was forever playing practical jokes. So it was that he came to stage one of his tricks at the mosque. The youngsters came to prayer one day, then a second and a third day. Their presence certainly did not go unnoticed. The old men, overcome with joy at the sight of their offspring becoming religious, congratulated them. The Imam devoted a sermon to them on the heavenly rewards awaiting them in the after-life. Under this mask of piety, Mbengue, at the end of a prayer, when one of the faithful went out to get a kettle or pot full of water, would rush out into the narrow corridor, and occupy the toilet. Several minutes of waiting would pass. The old man, tortured by his pressing needs, would bang on the door of the booth, as if to say: 'Hurry up in there. You aren't the only one.' The gang of youngsters, highly amused, would chuckle, and peer at the latrines. Waiting patiently, the old man would stamp his feet, move around, and then renew his plea: 'Hurry up!'

From inside, Mbengue could spy on the fidgeting man through a crack in the door. Beads of perspiration started appearing on his forehead and neck. Suffering keenly from his cramps, the man hammered on the door: 'I'm waiting!' Using his imagination, Mbengue put his forearm between his lips and blew. Incongruous sounds issued forth, and Mbengue, intending to make himself heard, said over and over in a loud voice: 'Allahou Akbar! Allahou Akbar! Allahou Akbar!' Mortified at having been the unwitting witness to such an intimate moment, the old man hastily took himself off somewhere else, far away. Exchanging furtive winks, the gang laughed together. This game continued for about a fortnight before the old people realized what was going on. They were outraged at the young boys' total lack of respect for their elders. The Imam spoke of the end of the world being almost upon them. The toilets were put out of bounds to all boys, since it was not possible to excommunicate them.

For weeks after this escapade, the boys laughed themselves silly.

The morning light, like a tranquil sea, was unveiling patches of colour. The young sun showed its claws.

Five carts carrying bricks went past one after another. Half-starved horses strained at their heavy load, grinding wheels sank into the black soil. The drivers, on foot, were forcing the old nags forward with repeated cracks of their whips.

Taaw, together with his two followers, appeared on the corner just left of the *essencerie*[1] and crossed the intersection which was already swarming with people, fast-buses[2] and beggars. The general din was growing louder and louder. As they came down the gentle slope, Mbengue put out both his arms and stopped his friends. He looked right, then left, and said, 'Boy, the usual ...'

The three looked at each other. Pointing with his chin, Mbengue gave the go-ahead.

'Okay, Boy', Taaw consented.

Mam Ass approached the doughnut-seller, who was balancing his tray on his head; Mbengue came up on the right. They engaged the vendor in small talk, while Taaw crept up from behind. Because of his height, he was able to sneak the doughnuts one after the other, in time with each step, and to stuff them into his pockets. Then he overtook his accomplices.

'Hey you, where did you get your flour?' Mbengue demanded in the dry tone of a policeman, catching hold of the vendor's arm. And without giving him a chance to reply, he declared: 'I'm sure your flour has come from the stocks intended for the peasants. Do you have a receipt?' And his bloodshot eyes fixed the vendor's in a cold stare.

Blinking nervously, his face dark with apprehension, the vendor looked from Mbengue to Mam Ass.

'We heard last night of a truck delivering flour. Give us your boss's address,' said Mam Ass.

'I'm only a retailer,' the young vendor uttered.

'Who do you work for? Who is your supplier?'

Mbengue's leopard outfit scared the dealer out of his wits, and

Translator's note: [1] petrol pump; lexical creation in West African French, from the French 'essence', petrol. [2] mini-bus taxis privately run in many parts of Africa.

he fell silent.

'He's just a poor devil,' Mam Ass said to Mbengue. 'Tell your boss that the police are looking into it.'

'*Moot! Moot!*' ordered Mbengue, when he had released the boy's arm. Pointing his finger, he forced him to retrace his steps.

Once he was a fair distance away, holding the tray of doughnuts firmly on his head, he turned around only to see Mbengue's finger still pointing at him. He did not wait for any more, but turned hastily off the road.

The three friends shared out the pilfered doughnuts among themselves as they carried on walking.

Above the entrance stood the words 'Branch Labour Office', in black letters. At the end of a narrow alley were three prefabricated buildings in which American troops had been quartered between 1943 and 1946, and which had been painted over for every new use to which they had been put. The doors opened onto each other and the windows served as counters for different trades and occupations. Men and women would sit and chat along the length of the verandas, while others lined up in front of the windows.

A young woman with a large rump was stating her case, gesturing emphatically with her hands.

'I've been working for this woman for four months, from morning till night. Yesterday she threw me out without paying me. I've been to the police. They told me to come here.'

At her side, her companion was punctuating each sentence with a rhythmic cadence of throaty sounds.

'Lady, this isn't the right place. Go to the Inspector of Work.' Diallo, the ledger clerk, dispensed advice from behind his table.

Behind him, cool air was being blown from a rotating fan on a stand.

'I've been to the Inspector, at the Trade Union. They wanted to see my pay-slip. My employer never gave me any papers. I don't have any payslip. But all the shopkeepers in the area know that I worked for this woman.'

'We can do nothing for you here,' was Diallo's pronouncement.

'For eight months now, our boss hasn't paid either of us. It's a construction firm. The boss filed a statement of liquidation and declared bankruptcy,' said one of the two men standing next to her. He was wearing a white caftan and a brown cap on his head.

'Who were you working for?' asked the other man, dressed in blue with a white cotton scarf around his neck

'For Oulimata Yandé. The big stone house you see as you get onto the main road,' the plaintiff eagerly answered, with wide eyes.

Her whole face radiated the innocence and naïveté of the country girl.

'You can be lucky. Almost all the maids who work for Oulimata Yandé land up in jail. She accuses them of stealing her jewels and her money,' said Diallo.

He caught sight of Taaw climbing the stairs, and shouted at him: 'Hey, boy.'

The two men turned around to see the trio coming towards them.

'*Koy!*' the woman exclaimed, slapping her thigh; she stared at her companion. 'I won't sweat for some slut,' she said in her mother tongue, which the others could not understand; then she went on in Wolof: 'I'm going to show that bitch a thing or two.'

She walked off determinedly, dragging the other woman with her.

'What times we live in!' remarked one of the men.

'How's it going, Diallo boy?' Taaw greeted; and seeing the two men: 'You're ahead of me.'

'We're waiting,' the man in the scarf told him, standing aside.

'How you doing, Taaw boy?'

'Fine.'

'And otherwise? Things going all right?'

'Fine, *Tonton* Gaston, everything's fine,' Taaw said casually, leaning his elbow on the counter.

Three clerks shared the cramped space. Dusty files were piled high in wooden cupboards with no doors. An interleading door opened onto a second room. Light fell from a neon lamp on the wall onto the edge of a red wooden table and a well-worn greenish carpet.

'People without trade or profession are not classified as unemployed,' *Tonton* Gaston quipped from his desk.

The telephone rang in the office next door. A deep, imposing voice was heard.

'Hello! Hello! Yes, speaking …'

Tonton Gaston sneaked a quick look at the office next door, and moved towards the window, edging his way between the tables. Close-cropped hair flecked with grey, safari shirt with a black band on its lapel, the sign of mourning in the Catholic Church. The director's loud voice resounded.

'Yes!… Yes!… I can hardly hear you! Yes!… Wait. Let me write this down … I'm listening!… Two skilled fitters. Good. A bookkeeper with experience. Police record. Please repeat that. Excellent. Twenty bricklayers for Gabon … Good!… Leaving in two weeks' time …'

The chap in the white scarf appeared in the window. Craning his neck so that he could see him, Taaw whispered to *Tonton* Gaston: 'Gaston, we all heard that. The director is talking about bricklayers needed in Gabon.'

'And you know how they choose workers for these jobs,' the other man said to Gaston, as he came up and stood next to Mbengue.

'You know what the boss is like. He is cautious and doesn't like to be rushed. That's the new generation for you.'

'Gaston, if we don't get this one, it's finished for our families. I promise you, we won't be ungrateful.'

'Come on, chap, what's wrong with you? If you have the right to go to Gabon, demand it without grovelling like that', Mbengue heatedly broke in.

The two men were irritating him.

The two workers were speechless, as though struck dumb by a thunderbolt, so stunned were they by Mbengue's outburst. Recovering from his amazement, the second man grabbed Mbengue by the throat and shouted at him:

'Who do you think you are, you little shit, to lecture us? At home. I've got five mouths to feed and clothe and shelter, the same age as you. I'm sure you're just like them, and do nothing to help your father. You don't go and fetch water, to help your mother and your sister. Do you ever pick up a spade to fill in the holes in your house? At your age, you are still fed and clothed and given a roof over your head. Who are you to talk about honesty and integrity?'

As the worker raged on, his grip on Mbengue's throat was becoming tighter and tighter. Mbengue started choking, his tongue hanging out.

'Samba! Samba, calm down,' the other man intervened, loosening the iron grip of his fingers.

'Father, forgive him. Forgive him in Yallah's name,' said Taaw, pushing Samba's hand away.

Mbengue was spluttering, tears streaming from his eyes. Mam Ass led him away.

'See if their names are down.'

Diallo opened a ledger with a black cover. 'They're at the top of the list: Babacar Samba and Ismaïla Diagne, skilled masons.'

'Keep quiet now. Especially you, Samba,' said *Tonton* Gaston; then to Taaw: 'Take this note, and go to the harbour. You'll find a man there called Bachirou.'

'I'd prefer to go to Gabon, *Tonton*. There's more money there. Don't forget that my wife is expecting our first child.'

Tonton Gaston pushed up his silver-framed glasses with his forefinger, in his habitual way. He said in a protective voice:

'Taaw, you don't have any qualifications to get you onto the list. They don't want unskilled labour in Gabon. Now do you want to go and see Bachirou or not?'

Feeling unsure of what to do, Taaw glanced around the room.

'*Tonton*,' interrupted Diallo, who had finally got up from his chair, '*Tonton*, this Bachirou needs something to help him understand, before he'll oblige anybody.'

There was silence.

'My son, listen to me carefully,' began Samba, facing Taaw. 'My son, I have heard you talking about your wife who has honoured you. If it pleases Yallah, you will soon be a father. Remember that by giving a handful of seed, (he closed his hand), you will fill your granary with enough to delight your family and your friends; and you will feel like a man ...' he ended off, very impressed by his own words.

'*Monsieur* Gaston!' the director called out from the other office.

'Yes, sir,' Gaston answered, holding out the note to Taaw: 'Find at least a thousand francs.* That's what will help him understand.'

Taking the piece of paper, Taaw went to join his two friends They went out together.

'That old fart can be lucky! I could have messed him up,' Mbengue swaggered, smoothing down his combat outfit.

'Boy, you going to grease someone's palm so you can get work? You really disappoint me, boy,' said Mam Ass.

'I'd do even more than that to get a job. Soon I'm going to be a father ... And I want to leave home,' Taaw explained.

'You're an arsehole, boy ... But you do it in style, I must say! You've hit the jackpot. Your father-in-law to be, Goor Yummbul, has got plenty. You really think he'll kick you out?... That he'll throw his daughter out onto the street?...'

'Never,' agreed Mam Ass.

'Your father-in-law will take you into his concession. He'll put you up with his daughter. And if you haven't got a job, is that your fault?'

'I don't think like you.'

---

* Author's note: one thousand francs C.F.A. (Communauté Financière Africaine)

'Boy, you really are an arsehole. But not a small-time one. Your father-in-law will proudly bounce his grandson on his knees. And from time to time, he'll even give you some pocket money, you'll see.'

'No, I don't think like you.'

'That old saying is true. The oldest son is either super smart or super stupid. As for you, you're as thick as a chamber pot.'

'Thanks. *Ciao.*'

Yaye Dabo was becoming more and more alarmed by the arguments between her oldest son and her husband. She was resigned to the domestic scenes between husband and wife, but the open hostility between father and son went beyond her comprehension. When Taaw was in prison, Baye Tine had left the house and quite openly gone to live with his second wife. She had appealed to the Imam, the community's moral centre, in the hope that her husband would resume his *môrné*. If not for her sake, as his wife, at least for the children and also because of the neighbours. On her knees, she had begged Baye Tine to forgive her. After the elders had approached him, Baye Tine had taken up again his conjugal rotations. After her son's release, Yaye Dabo made a concerted effort to keep her home peaceful and in order: she was always available, acquiescent, and sympathetic to her husband's complaints.

That morning the situation had reached breaking point. She strongly felt the need to keep Taaw away from his father. After Baye Tine had left, she hurriedly rinsed his trousers and hung them out on the line to dry. She had smeared Abdou's buttocks with karité butter before sending him off to the Daraa.

'Dabo! Dabo!' called a woman's voice.

'Soumaré! Soumaré, queen of Nglam ...,' answered Yaye Dabo.

'I see it's your *môrné*,' said the Soumaré* in a friendly voice,

---

* Translator's note: her name is Soumaré. 'The' is an affectionate usage, implying that she is well known and respected.

the handle of her red plastic bucket hooked over her forearm.

'Rather say you heard Abdou crying when his father was thrashing him. As for me, I no longer need to purify myself when I get out of bed,' Yaye Dabo replied, with a bitter note of complaint in her voice.

'Dabo, you're not going to tell me that you've given "it" up already,' said Soumaré in a gently teasing voice, checking the suggestive gesture she was making.

'I fatten him up for my young co-wife,' Yaye Dabo confided, forcing a bitter smile.

'Ey! Yaye Dabo, don't we all.'

'But it's true. All I'm good for is the bedside mat ...'

Soumaré laughed, displaying a fine set of teeth.

'Don't go and buy vegetables. I've got some very fresh ones.'

'Sure thing! Let me get going before I melt in the sun.'

In the yard a little girl was doing the washing, leaning her head on her shoulder. Music was playing on the radio next to her, and her hands were working in time to the beat. Yaye Dabo took out the short table which served as a counter for the condiments she had for sale. As Baye Tine gave her only twelve thousand francs* a month for her three sons, she ran this small business to supplement her household income.

Taaw came running in.

'Is the country burning down?' she asked, surprised.

Taaw, panting, held his forehead. He bent down, with his hands on his knees.

'Mother, I need a thousand francs.'

'*Reek!* A thousand francs,' she repeated ironically. 'And where do you think I'm going to find a thousand francs?'

'Mother, it's a bribe I need for someone who's going to get me a job.'

Yaye Dabo sat down on the little bench. Taaw crouched in front of her, resting his hand on her knee and looking lovingly at her. The mother was moved, and turned her eyes from him to

* Author's note: twelve thousand francs C.F.A.

the little girl doing the washing.

For years now she had wanted to confide in someone, even if only her son. To speak about her household, her husband, and her children's future. Ever since they had moved to this suburb, she had been her husband's doormat. During the day, Baye Tine would take up his *mômé*, but in private, he refused to carry out his conjugal duties – and this had been going on for three years. The first month it happened, she had complained to the Imam. The outcome was even more painful and humiliating: that night, Baye Tine hurled torrents of abuse at her so vulgar that she had broken out in a sweat … a bitch on heat, he called her. And one night, she had been chased from the bed. With all intercourse between herself and her husband broken off, she spent the night of her *mômé* on a mat on the floor at the foot of the bed, covered with a loincloth. She had never breathed a word of this to anyone. She accepted all the suffering that her husband inflicted on her, so that her children might succeed in life. Is that not the lot of the woman, of the wife? So she had been told. So it is believed.

'Mother, why are you crying?' Taaw asked, his forehead creased in a frown.

At the corners of his mouth, two manly lines were beginning to appear: 'Mother, I've only got seventy-five francs.'

Yaye Dabo wiped her tears with her long shirt. Standing up, she unpegged Baye Tine's trousers and felt the wet patch before folding them up.

'Taaw,' she said in a soft voice, 'if it really is to get work, sell these,'

'Mother! Those are my father's trousers!'

'I know that better than you do.' She forced the trousers into his hands.

Taaw walked away with measured steps.

Just outside the concession, an enormous baobab in the middle of the untarred road blocked out the horizon, creating a natural traffic circle. Barriers of concrete, wood and galvanized iron lined the road on either side, broken here and there by streets and alleys. Groups of young girls in the same age group and from the same village walked past briskly in the hope of finding jobs as maids. The warm, bright, daring colours of their outfits shimmered like a bed of nodding flowers. Empty cans and broken glass bottles glinted here and there, catching the slanting rays of the rising sun. The hubbub was growing steadily louder.

'Taaw,' called Astou, coming to meet him.

A smile lit her whole face, and her hands made a half-movement. 'I saw you running into your house. I hope nothing's wrong,' she said, looking up at him.

'Nothing serious! I wanted to borrow a thousand francs from my mother. Can you believe it, I'm going to have to pay somebody to give me a job,' Taaw replied, taking her hands in his.

'She lent you the money?'

'No! But she suggested that I sell my father's trousers instead. And where are you going?'

Astou looked suddenly apprehensive.

'I'm going to the Family Planning Clinic,' she answered and then speaking rapidly: 'Taaw, a son should never sell his father's trousers – that brings bad luck. Think of our child.'

Moving her elbows and wrists, she gathered up her large sky-blue boubou, pushing its folds under her armpits. She opened her handbag and, taking out two five-hundred franc notes, handed them to Taaw. She smiled. Taaw held the generous hand in his, caressing it with his thumb.

Astou Ngom was seventeen and a half years old.

Their romance had started more than four years ago. They believed that they had invented their own invisible language, more sensitive than any other, which allowed them to have contact and to live out their demanding and intense relationship. When they met in public, they would brush lightly against each other, and smile. Their hearts' silent voices found expression in looks, gestures and smiles. As their hearts opened to each other, so their desire to touch each other grew stronger.

Their first union took place on the night of Mawloud, the birthday of the prophet Mohamadou Rassoulillahi. In the deepest moment of the night, in the tumult of the chanting, the young people slipped off together as many other couples were doing. No longer frightened of parents or concerned about other people, they loved each other freely. After this, they met in all sorts of different places.

'I waited for you the other day at Adama's', said Taaw.

His thumb was stroking, up and down.

'We're being watched.'

Taaw looked up and met the gaze of the shoemaker who kept shop under the baobab. He withdrew his hand. They devoured each other with their eyes before going their separate ways.

Neither Astou nor Taaw had yet given much thought to how their parents would react. But Astou knew that her father, Aladji Ngom, nicknamed Goor Yummbul, was aware of her pregnancy.

After three months and several suns, Astou had disclosed her condition to her mother, Sohna, in the latter's room. For a moment, the mother remained frozen. Then, as though she was demented, she threw herself at Astou and, fumbling under her daughter's loincloth, fiercely grabbed her crotch. Astou screamed.

'You got it in through here and I'm going to get it out the same way ...'

Astou's screams brought the three other co-wives running in. They had to struggle to unprise Sohna's hand which was clawing at her daughter's flesh, her fingertips and nails spotted with blood.

'I'll kill this slut,' Sohna was crying over and over, beside herself with rage, while the first and second wives restrained her.

The fourth wife took Astou to her quarters, to keep her under her protection. It was a rule agreed to among the co-wives that none of them had the right to go after her children if they had sought refuge with one of the other wives. Safe from her mother's violent attacks, Astou confessed to her other mothers. Sohna, whose hopes as a mother had been dashed, was reviling her daughter. She could see herself mocked and hounded by the jeers of the co-wives and all the women in the neighbourhood. The entire female population would laugh at her behind her back. For days, her anger did not abate.

The first wife, the *doyenne*, already past fifty, called the other three together: Nafissatou the second, Sohna the third, and the fourth, Bineta.

'Let us accept this trial as a divine sign. After all, it affects all of us. The real problem is our husband. How are we going to tell him the truth before he finds it out in the street?'

The *doyenne*, who knew her husband's weak spot, suggested they wait for the most favourable opportunity before breaking the news of Astou's pregnancy to him. All agreed to avoid their night-time conjugal duties.

Astou returned to her mother's quarters.

Aladji Ngom did not go unnoticed in the neighbourhood. A lear old man in his seventies, he had small piercing eyes full of mis·hief; his white goatee trimmed to a point was the only van ty that he allowed himself. He used to be a driver. When he retired, he acquired a second-hand Peugeot van and wrote above the windscreen, in black the Arabic script, and in red the Latin, for GOOR YUMMBUL ('It is hard to be a man.'). Proud of this nickname assumed during his adolescence, he had finally lived up to it. A beast of burden, he had built his own concession – and it was a large one – and had walled it around. Father of twenty-eight children, he had four wives, each of whom occupied her own part of the house. He had arranged for himself his own universe, and when it was her *mômé*, each wife would come and spend three nights with him. As he was of the old school, the women and children came to pay him their respects as soon as he got home from work at the end of each day.

That night Sohna, Astou's mother, made herself beautiful, so that her *môme* would be perfectly consummated. She had redone her plaits, her palms and heels were dyed with henna, and she wore a light, see-through blouse with a neck low enough to reveal her well-rounded shoulders; a valuable handwoven cloth moulded her hips. Her body was perfumed, and incense filled the room. During the intimate meal for two, she mischievously teased the old man with seemingly innocent gestures, bold language and studied abandon, in order to arouse his desire. At the same time, she was surreptitiously keeping a close watch on him, and a few times caught the glint of desire in Goor Yummbul's eye. Knowing that he had been starved of sex for some days, she flitted about around him.

Aladji, relaxed, was feeling light-hearted and buoyant. After the meal, he stretched out on the couch as usual, enjoying a Xalam solo, the music he enjoyed most after the reading of the Koran.

Sohna got Astou to come in behind her. They took their places on the mat. Astou kept behind her mother, her fear draped over her like a cloak.

'*Nidiaye!*'* Sohna whispered.

Calmly, the old man turned to look at them. His little eyes lighted first on the one, and then on the other. Astou, feeling his searching gaze upon her, turned to ice.

'I'm listening,' he said.

'We have been tainted with shame. Astou is expecting ...'

Aladji lifted a scrawny arm to turn down the volume.

'What were you saying?'

'Astou has sinned.'

'Which Astou?'

The question stunned Sohna, the mother. She was distraught, but made an immense effort to control herself. A burning sensa-

* Author's note: Uncle. When used by the wife: 'darling', or 'my lord'.

tion shot through her body and her mouth contorted in a nervous twitch. A drop of sweat trickled its way down her spine.

'Astou Ngom, my daughter.'

The words tumbled out, and she swallowed hard. Then, her face radiant with tenderness, she turned to her daughter who was stifling her groans. The gold chain around the mother's neck gleamed, striking against her black skin.

The liquid notes of the Xalam were pouring into the room, reminiscent of those days when men were still heroes. Only the wall of silence echoed back, like a raging tornado taking endless agonising seconds to coil itself up.

'Does she at least know ...'

Goor Yummbul refused to complete his sentence. As he crossed his arms over his chest, his gaze lingered on his wife...

'It's Taaw,' Sohna hastened to reply. And in a sudden rush of words, she felt it wise to add: 'Taaw, the oldest son of Baye Tine and Yaye Dabo. Their house is just behind here. They aren't lower caste. They are respectable folk. You ...'

'*Doy na!* That's enough!' the man barked out.

These two words went through the woman's heart like a sharp blade.

The silence hung heavy in the thick atmosphere.

The man lifted his eyes to the ceiling. In the naked light, the hard lines of his face stood out, and his goatee appeared unnaturally white.

Repeated coughing and scraping sounds told Sohna that outside the room her co-wives were supporting her. For days on end, they had tried to predict what the husband's questions would be, and to work out what answers to give him. Sohna had expected Goor Yummbul to shout, curse, storm, and even beat her. Her strategy had crumbled. Faced with the silence and the man's composure, she was losing control of the situation. She was humiliated by the harsh command he had given her in her daughter's presence. At that moment she would rather have committed infanticide, than suffer such shame.

Astou, who was prostrate, suddenly clutched her hands to her mouth.

'Put it back where it came from,' the father ordered, pointing at Astou.

'Don't you vomit here,' he added.

Her cheeks puffed out, she pressed her hands against her mouth. The liquid started oozing out between her fingers. She was going through agony.

'Swallow it,' the father repeated firmly.

Sohna felt sorry for her daughter. She watched her gulp down mouthful after mouthful.

'Have you spoken to anyone else about this?' he asked, his face impassive.

He seemed to be groping for an elusive idea.

'*Nidiaye*, would I dare to parade our shame before anyone else?' Sohna returned vehemently, raising her hand as though taking an oath.

Goor Yummbul let out a quivering sneer, loaded with irony. 'Love a woman, but never trust her,' he thought to himself, remembering the words of the sage. He was convinced that his household, the neighbours, the people in the street and in the entire neighbourhood, all knew of his shame. He was known and respected in the area and had a position to maintain.

'Tell *your daughter* to get out.'

Sohna patted Astou's knee. With one hand holding her mouth, Astou used the other one to press herself up from the ground. She almost fell, and steadied herself by leaning on her mother's head. Sohna stood up quickly to support the weight of her daughter's body. This succession of gestures and movements which bore witness to some invisible bond, incensed the old man. Sohna's eyes followed Astou's bare feet as they padded out.

As soon as Astou had escaped, she vomited.

The murmuring of women's voices was heard.

In the silent lounge, the music was overpowering. Sohna, her eyes downcast, smoothed out the edges of her loincloth.

Aladji Ngom, alias Goor Yummbul, prided himself on belonging to a family of noble descent. An untainted line had passed down from generation to generation the highest virtues and principles. Never had the Ngoms made their way by the use of force or perfidy, or through the desire for gain, or in the pursuit of fame. He himself lived and struggled only for his family. He had given them the best of himself. Four of his sons had gone into exile ... Two daughters had married men of low social standing, which he could not accept. Was he questioning the meaning of his life? His sacrifice? He had reaped nothing but bitterness. His self-respect and pride had been wounded once again, and he was regretting all the years that he had slaved for them. He found no answer to any of his questions. He took refuge in the distant past, where he found comfort, and from where he condemned the values of the present.

'Is my bed ready?' he asked, his voice thick with reproach.

'Yes, *Nidiaye*.'

With accusing eyes fixed on the woman, he stood up to go to his bedroom. Once he had closed the door and switched off the lights, Sohna joined him in bed. The subtle exhalation of her perfume excited the man's senses, and aroused his desire. The contact of his body with the woman's caused a conflict between desire, willpower, and the state of his nerves. After two weeks of deprivation, he had felt a fleeting urge when he woke up that morning.

During the day, Goor Yummbul's thoughts had inadvertently turned to 'it'. He had also puzzled over the behaviour of three of his wives during their *môme*. During the meal, he had responded to Sohna's teasing play. His eyes had been arrested by the fullness and beauty of the woman's rounded shoulders. Her skin, black as night, made the gold chain around her neck stand out, sparkling as it caught the light. Each of her graceful, feminine movements gave off a soft fragrance of gongo.* The old

* Translator's note: a type of incense, crushed into a powder. It is placed in little bags against the skin, under a dress or loincloth.

man was seduced by all these charms, and had savoured, in anticipation, the pleasures that were awaiting him. His desire was awakened ... sublime feeling!

The revelation of his daughter's condition stopped short his inner urge. Like water through a crack in a dam wall, the unpleasant news invaded his being drop by drop, until it petrified his joints, blocking in him all desire to make love.

With a sudden rough, aggressive movement, the old man pushed away Sohna's knee which was brushing lightly against him, and turned his back to her.

During the following suns, Goor Yummbul's relentless silence kept his four wives and the children on tenterhooks. An atmosphere of mourning hung over them. Aladji Ngom-Goor Yummbul was deaf to any conversation, word, or sign. This distance he imposed, and his refusal to honour his wives, frightened and alarmed all. Everyone was expecting some violent outbreak, but it never came. Perhaps the man, growing old, and worn out by the daily struggle for his family's wellbeing, was bowing down to the storm inside him, waiting for it to pass. In the concession, the tension of fear subsided as the days went by. Wives and children resumed their humdrum lives. Astou no longer hid her very obvious pregnancy, and she came with the others to greet her father at the end of each day.

Weeks later, Aladji Ngom took up the issue with Baye Tine. They were on their way back from a funeral service.

'One of my daughters has been "wronged",' began Goor Yummbul as soon as they were out of the cemetery.

'Han!' Baye Tine exclaimed walking with his potbelly protruding. 'What times we live in! I know how you feel. These days children have no respect for their parents' honour. You work yourself into the ground to give them food and clothes and a roof over their heads, and they drag your name in the dirt with their shameless acts.'

Some faithfuls overtook them.

'My daughter says that it's your son Taaw who is the

"craftsman".'

Baye Tine stopped short, and stared at Goor Yummbul's neck. 'Did you say Taaw?'

'Yes, your son Taaw,' Goor Yummbul replied, looking straight into Baye Tine's eyes as the latter caught up with him.

For a while Baye Tine said nothing, allowing his eyes to wander.

'*Amine! Amine!* May Yallah grant divine mercy to the deceased and may he keep us all alive by taking us under his all-powerful protection. May he help us every day,' Goor Yummbul proclaimed to the world at large, for the benefit of a passing group of men escorting the local chief and the Imam. They answered in chorus: '*Amine! Amine!*' as they went on their way.

'So what have you got to say about it?' the seventy-year-old demanded of Baye Tine, a man of sixty-three, as though he were a child.

'Taaw has nothing. He has nothing to put in his stomach, let alone to cover his backside with ...'

From behind white lashes which looked like a curtain of cotton threads, Goor Yummbul's narrowed eyes haughtily scanned Baye Tine's face.

'Neither his mother nor Taaw has confided in me,' Baye Tine said in justification, trying to dodge the question.

He said to himself that Aladji was trying to find a father for his daughter's child, to save face. He said in conclusion: 'It happens that girls, in the confusion of this kind of predicament, pin the blame onto a man who ...'

'Are you disputing what I say?' Goor Yummbul demanded, irritated by Baye Tine's insinuations.

'I haven't finished, Aladji.'

In this township, everybody knew what everybody else was up to. Baye Tine had the reputation of being a profiteer and a liar of the first order. Already, Goor Yummbul felt contempt for this man. The thought of him as a future in-law filled him with bitterness. Without another word, he left Baye Tine.

The tugboat's sharp whistle could be heard repeatedly in the distance. Out at sea, between Goree Island and the jetty – a stony arm extending out into the sea – a steamer glided over the water. A strong, low wind ruffled the surface, whipping up small silver-crested waves. The launch which served to link the island and the mainland started pitching as it reached the open sea.

The heavy traffic at the entrance to the docks was being regulated by policemen and customs officials, and idlers, swindlers and dealers swarmed around in a seething mass. A strong, persistent smell, a combination of the stench of rancid oil, refuse thrown up by the ocean and rotten fish, assailed the nostrils. The vibrations of a pneumatic drill added to the din of engines, cars and motorbikes.

Bachirou, a celebrity around the docks, was not difficult to find. He had his office out in the open, under a snack-bar canopy. Wearing an embroidered, white-striped grey caftan and a red fez, his eyes hidden behind dark glasses, he was sitting with one arm leaning on the metal table, an attaché-case and a half-empty cup of coffee in front of him. Behind the glasses, his darting eyes kept a close watch on the entrance to the quays. Taaw stood in line waiting his turn. Twice, Bachirou had gone into the enclosed area of the quays and walked out again as though from his own lounge. On familiar terms with the policemen, the customs officials and the drivers, he chatted away enthusiastically.

'Okay *petit*, you're next,' said Bachirou after shaking hands with his last two clients.

Once he had read the note, he carefully looked Taaw up and down.

'*Tonton* Gaston sent me. I've got my elementary diploma.'

Bachirou smiled at him. Or rather, he pulled his mouth so that he looked like someone in the know.

'Take a seat, *petit*,' he invited, condescending. ' You must know, *petit*, these days it's more difficult to get a job than a wife.

People with B.A.s, engineers, doctors, nobody's got jobs. Not to mention all the skilled workers just sitting around. There's nothing you're qualified for … And you've never worked.'

'It's true, *Grand-bi**, but I have to find work. My wife is expecting our first child,' Taaw said, pleading his case.

'I like your honesty … Youssou! Youssou! Wait, I want to talk to you.'

Bachirou briskly walked over to Youssou who was dressed in a red and yellow-striped boubou. He had a thick neck, with rolls of fat. Taaw watched the two men conversing at a distance.

'So, *petit, Tonton* Gaston put you in the know?' Bachirou asked when he came back.

'Yes,' Taaw replied, slipping him the two five-hundred-franc notes.

Bachirou openly checked the money before pocketing it.

'It's for your file. With your diploma you could be an assistant plasterer, with a good chance of being promoted. Is that a pair of trousers you've got there?'

'Yes, they're my uncle's. I have to go to the tailor,' Taaw replied, not knowing why he lied. Then, he pleaded: 'Help me, *Grand-bi*. You won't be sorry,' he ended off, repeating exactly what he had heard a mason saying to *Tonton* Gaston at the Labour Office.

'These are the conditions. I find you a job, you sign an 'i.o.u.': a quarter of your monthly salary for five months. It's to help you.'

'I'll go along with that, *Grand-bi*. A quarter of my salary for five months.'

'That's it, *petit*. Be here tomorrow morning at half-past five.'
'Tomorrow?'

'Yes, tomorrow. By the way, what's your name?'
'Taaw.'

Bachirou scratched the word 'Taaw' in Arabic letters on his left palm, and tapped his forehead.

* Translator's note: Grand-bi = Bi = term used to address an elder.

Taaw left with the trousers, his heart filled with hope and joy. On the gates of three workshops he read: 'No vacancies.' He laughed. How many times hadn't he read those signs! How many times had his heart not ached! A flood of disappointment had swept over him every time. It had been his ambition to study computer science. He held it against his father that he had been expelled from school. As the years went by, the anger he felt towards his father had grown to such an extent that the thought of killing him sometimes crossed his mind. He saw his father, a wreck, relentlessly battering his mother. Tomorrow he would start working! His thoughts turned to Astou, and to his mother. His father would be proud of him, and respect him. And he, Taaw, would show him the door ... Yes, he would throw his father out. Yaye Dabo would intervene and say to him: 'Taaw, this is your father, my husband. You can't put him out like a dog.' And he, a responsible man, would say to his father: 'You can be grateful to my mother! When I was very small, you took the bursary awarded to me by the State, to go off and take a second wife. And our house in the médina, you squandered the money from that ... on your own pleasure.'

'Taaw, you do not speak to your father like that.'

The siren of an ambulance rushing past at full speed jolted Taaw out of his imagined monologue. Curious, his eyes followed the ambulance as it weaved its way through the cars. He looked around. Two young women in a stationary grey Toyota right opposite the harbour gate attracted his attention. One of the women, the one behind the steering-wheel, had skin the colour of pumpkin flesh, with lips, eyelashes and eyebrows lined cheekily with thick, shiny black. On her wrist she wore a dozen or so thin gold bracelets. She was tapping her fingers on the side rear-view mirror. The other one, who looked less de-pigmented – possibly because of the shadow in the car – also seemed to be on the look-out. She watched everything that was going on around them.

'The truck will be coming out soon,' the first one said, her eyes following a motor cycle.

'It's too risky to try to take it all out at once,' the second one replied, turning to her companion.

'Bachirou knows what he's doing. If he wants it all to come out at once, it's because he knows whoever's on duty. Bachirou is a man of his word. You ...'

The second one nudged her. Both stared at Taaw who was looking at them, more out of fascination than anything else. He continued on his way, repeating to himself the snippet of conversation which he had gleaned: 'Bachirou knows what he's doing.' He felt confident about his future. Tomorrow he would be working.

Taaw had made a promising start to his studies. He was a responsive pupil, and sailed through primary school. He was awarded his primary school diploma at the age of twelve, and went on to pass the entrance exam to the High School. This double success earned him a bursary and a number of prizes. The headmaster called Baye Tine in to congratulate him on raising his son so well. Baye Tine framed the diploma and hung it ostentatiously in his lounge. Yaye Dabo was not sparing in the praises she gave her son. Both father and mother could already see in Taaw the future supporter of the family, who would be their safeguard when they grew old.

The following year, in the middle of the school term, the family moved to the township. Taaw and his younger brother Souleymane had to travel eleven kilometres between home and school four times a day. They had been there for barely five weeks when Souleymane, who was nine years old, fell ill. He missed the rest of the year. Yaye Dabo had to cope with these problems alone: finding money for transport, nursing Souleymane, and also keeping an eye on Abdou who would drift off to the beach with the other young imps of his age. Baye Tine had just taken a second wife, and was squandering all the money they had saved by moving.

One night, in their candlelit bedroom, Yaye Dabo finally

found the courage to approach her husband about it. This was still before he had chased her out of bed.

'Baye, you must help me,' she said in a very gentle voice, fastening her nightcloth.

The flickering light of the candle threw her thick shadow against the wall.

'What have you been doing with the allowance I give you every month?' Baye Tine asked sternly, sitting on the edge of the bed, wearing nothing but an old faded gown.

The man knew his wife. Whenever she started with this whining tone, it was because she wanted to get something out of him.

'I can't cover the cost of the children's clothes, their food, and the medicines I need for Souleymane, all by myself ... Taaw has a bursary. You are pocketing that money ... as well as the family allowance. But his transport and stationery for school have still got to be paid for. I'm asking nothing, absolutely nothing, for myself.'

Baye Tine sat squarely on his buttocks. He tapped his one bent knee with a knowing air. He deliberately allowed some moments of silence to pass. Somewhere the beating of drums pierced the wall of night. Closer by, in the street, strains of modern music approached and then faded again.

'It's you who put that idea in their heads! Because you yourself need money.'

'No! No! Taaw told me so. And he told me to ask you. Taaw isn't stupid.'

'So I'm the one who's stupid?'

The cloth which Yaye Dabo wore tightly around her hair made her head look like a round ball. She crept to the far end of the bed. She couldn't express her secret thoughts for fear of arousing her husband's irritation.

'You tell Taaw to come and talk to me about it. Anything Taaw may own or possess belongs to me ...'

'We were paid compensation money for moving to this suburb. And I don't see how that money has helped us … me and the children?'

'*Ahan!* Now you're saying what you really mean. Do you know how much I cashed in?'

'You never told me.'

Baye Tine swung himself around, and stared straight at her. Yaye Dabo, lying on the bed with her back to him, moved further away from him and faced the wooden wall. She regretted having spoken at all.

'Now I have to report to you on everything I do, is that it? Who are you that I should be accountable to you? And justify what I do? Ey! Listen to me carefully … In this house, I'm the one who wears the trousers. The problem is that you're jealous. So you think I'm wasting my money on your co-wife? I knew you'd bring her into it.'

'Baye, it was very good that you took a second wife. All I want you to do is help me raise our children and make them men of the future. I'm sorry if I offended you … *Bal maa! Bal maa*, Tine,' she ended off.

Her eyes ran along the narrow slit between two badly-joined boards. She gently ran her hand over it. A fresh breeze licked over her skin.

'Tomorrow,' she said to herself, 'I'll fill it up.' She pulled up the covers.

Baye Tine was seething, even though she had touched his one sensitive spot. He took pride in being acknowledged as the master. A few days after that, he magnanimously gave money to Yaye Dabo, saying to her:

'You can see this as moral compensation for the grief that I'm causing you by taking a second wife.'

Yaye Dabo was deeply hurt by this. If she had not needed the money for her children, she would have refused it. She saved on transport at lunch-time by giving Taaw money to buy something to keep his hunger pangs at bay. At the end of the year, Taaw was amongst those who had to repeat the class. As for

Souleymane, he had been taken out of school because of the lack of money, and because they were waiting for a new primary school to open in the area ... All parents were supposed to contribute towards its building costs ... During the holidays Yaye Dabo made enquiries about a school closer by for Taaw, but there was no secondary school on the city outskirts. A few days before school re-opened, she went to see her brother Sakhaly Dabo, a tailor by trade.

The brother received his older sister into his spacious, ostentatiously furnished lounge, complete with refrigerator, colour television, heavy Empire period armchairs fitted with plastic covers in pale blue-and-yellow stripes, an abundance of photographs on the walls, and glass sideboard filled with trinkets.

'Ey! Yaye, you have come to scold me,' Sakhaly said, craning his neck because of the hump on his left shoulder.

This deformity was also the cause of a slight limp.

Yaye Dabo sat down in an armchair facing the front door. She undid the big white scarf wrapped around her headcloth.

'Your visit fills my heart with joy. You hadn't forgotten that on Fridays I come home to eat?'

'It's a heritage from our father. Every Friday, the whole family used to gather around him.'

'We did,' Sakhaly affirmed, as he sat down.

They reminisced about their childhood, until they were interrupted by Sakhaly's first wife, Aïda, coming in with the welcoming water. She made a deferential half genuflexion.

'Oldest of mothers, you must be exhausted by this heat. For weeks now we* have been begging Sakhaly to fix the refrigerator so that we can have some cold water.'

Her comment was heavy with reproach.

'You know that I got the repairmen in, and paid them to fix it. But we always end up back where we started. Every household in the neighbourhood uses this refrigerator. Do you know, Aïda, how much a new refrigerator of this size would cost?'

* Author's note: understand by 'we' herself and her co-wife.

All eyes turned to the bright white monster on its stand. Yaye Dabo noticed that the door was ajar. She was annoyed by the domestic quarrel starting up over something so trivial. She knew that her younger brother's wife completely dominated him.

'Public transport really is an ordeal. I was thrown around the whole way,' Yaye Dabo said as she handed the bowl of water back to Aïda. 'Thank you!... Thank you!... Kane*.'

'And my nephew Djibril Taaw? I'm his uncle, yet he doesn't even visit me. Doesn't he know that I have more authority over him than his father?' Sakhaly declared, demonstrating his verbal skill.

'Dabo, what you say is true ... But there's more to it than that.'

'Are you trying to punish us, oldest of mothers, because we haven't been to see you since you moved to the township? Is that why you deprive the uncle of his nephew?'

'Aïda, spare me please,' Yaye Dabo said, careful not to challenge Aïda in a field where she excelled. 'Until this morning, I didn't even know that I was coming to see you. I've come to get school supplies for Taaw and for Souleymane ... Abdou is going to the Daraa.'

'Give me the list I'll buy those things.' Sakhaly stretched out his arm.

A little girl of about nine or ten spread out a new mat while the first wife brought a bowl of golden rice, fried and garnished with grouper and vegetables.

'Oldest of mothers, if I had dreamed that you might be coming, I would have slaughtered a sheep in your honour,' Aïda said, handing Yaye Dabo the finger-bowl. 'Come, oldest of mothers ... there ...'

Yaye Dabo washed her hands.

Sakhaly took his usual place in one of the armchairs. '*Bissimilahi,*' he pronounced. The meal was animated by talk of various issues in their lives. Aïda directed the small-talk, supporting

* Author's note: Aïda's family name.

now her sister-in-law, now her husband. She avoided meeting Yaye Dabo's eyes.

'I haven't seen my co-wife yet,' Yaye Dabo stated, by way of changing the conversation.

'She makes herself beautiful, like all second wives, on the day of their *môhé*.'

Yaye Dabo did not know what to make of this remark. Was Aïda alluding to the fact that Baye Tine had taken a second wife?

'The *awa** is queen in the home,' Yaye Dabo replied, washing her hands again at the end of the meal.

'Oh! I, you know, oldest of mothers, I do not try to compete anymore. I have given to you the seed which Yallah planted in my loins.'

'Truly, you have brought honour to our name. I pray that Yallah may grant the children a life filled with happiness and that they will help us through the hardships of old age.'

'*Amine! Amine!* Queen of mothers,' repeated Aïda, removing the container which the little girl had obediently come to fetch.

Sakhaly rinsed his hands and went one better with his '*Amine! Amine! Ya Rabi.*' Then, with one hard bite, he cracked open the cola nut to give a piece to Yaye Dabo. He crunched noisily.

'Sakhaly, I want to speak to you, and in Aïda's presence.'

'I can leave, ' Aïda declared, looking stern as she made to go, pushing herself up from the floor.

Yaye Dabo held her back, placing her hand over Aïda's.

'Do not misunderstand me. This concerns you. We live far, very far away from Taaw's school. Last year, he didn't do well in class because of the distances he had to travel. This coming and going four times a day is too much for a young boy. I would like it if he could come and have his lunches here. To tell you the truth, this is the reason why I am here.'

'Ey! Yaye, you make me sad. You don't have to ask us. Am I not Djibril's uncle? and Aïda his aunt?'

* Translator's note: first wife.

Sakhaly's question hung in the air. Again he was using a strong tone of voice to assert himself.

'Queen of mothers, you are our elder. Sakhaly is right,' Aïda added.

She was taking care to make a good impression on her sister-in-law.

Since Yaye Dabo had arrived, Aïda had been wondering what she could have come for. She had estranged Sakhaly from his friends and his family. The man's isolation made it so much easier for her to keep him under her thumb. She continued, very affably. 'These days children don't know their uncles, or their aunts, or their cousins. The only people they know are their mothers and fathers.'

'It's true, Kane,' said Yaye Dabo; she caught her brother's eyes looking to Aïda for approval.

'Dabo! Dabo!' came the piping voice of Anta Cissé, the second wife, as she came before Yaye Dabo and did a genuflexion.

She was wearing a large see-through tulle camisole which revealed her red brassière and her white loin-cloth decorated with thin red circles.

'Cissé! Cissé!' Yaye Dabo responded. 'I was beginning to think you were giving me the cold shoulder.'

'Yallah preserve me. Even if my heart told me to do so, my will would not obey, Dabo. Don't you see that I have made myself beautiful for you ...? Especially for you.'

'I see that and I forgive you.'

Then Yaye Dabo filled her in on the reason for her visit. The aunts agreed to the arrangements: Taaw would have a second family. Sakhaly got up.

'I must also get back,' said Yaye Dabo, following her brother.

The two sisters-in-law showed great generosity. Aïda gave Yaye Dabo three thousand francs, and Anta gave her a valuable new handwoven cloth.

Slowly, Taaw became a part of his uncle's family. The first term was a period of adjustment for him. He got to know all his cousins, and his two aunts. As for his uncle Sakhaly, he saw nothing of him. The latter was there only once a week, after the big Friday prayer once the children had already left for school. Aunt Aïda's two eldest children went to the same school as Taaw, and were two classes below him. At home, Taaw helped them with their homework. He shared their meals with them. It was a perfect environment for the development of young minds. Aunt Anta Cissé, the second wife, had become attached to Taaw. In return, Taaw looked after her child who was just starting school. And the formidable Aunt Aïda? Taaw was wary of her, and kept out of her way. A strong feeling of apprehension informed the way he behaved in her presence. For two months running, Taaw came first in his class. Yaye Dabo told her son to show his report to Aunt Aïda.

'Aunt, I came first again in my class,' Taaw came to tell her, showing her his marks.

Without looking at the piece of paper, Aïda frowned sternly at the pupil.

'You should be helping your cousins too.'

'But Aunt, I do help them,' Taaw protested.

Aunt Aïda's coarse face darkened. It was pinched and irritable, and stared contemptuously at Taaw. Taaw was vulnerable and felt torn apart. For a short moment, their eyes met. Taaw quickly looked away, more through alarm than politeness. Dragging his feet, humiliated, the child withdrew to the doob tree, taking his report with him.

As the days went by, Taaw noticed that all the members of the household were avoiding him. Usually he would come home with his cousins. Now, they were excluding him from their games, forming a new group without him, and crossing to the other side of the road if they saw him approaching. One day, standing in the doorway of the house, Aunt Aïda's eldest son Doudou mockingly asked him: 'Taaw, isn't there anything to eat at your father's house ...? You always eat at our house, why?' The question took Taaw by surprise and he was lost for an answer. He had a lump in his throat. The other cousins took up the chorus, chanting: 'Taaw the xarann cat. Taaw the sponger.' This taunting refrain hurt and angered Taaw. He went to his Aunt Anta who sent him to Aunt Aïda: 'Don't come and bother me with your childish stories. Go and sit under the doob.' As he walked off, he heard her say. 'After all, if that's what they're saying, it must be true.'

At midday, a fight broke out between Taaw and Doudou. Doudou claimed that Taaw had insulted his father and mother. Taaw tried in vain to deny this; Aïda nevertheless called him all sorts of names: 'Ungrateful brat ... When we feed you ... Look at you ... You've grown fat as a bull ...' Meanwhile, the other aunt had removed her offspring, so that they wouldn't hear all this.

Taaw's isolation increased during the following suns. Aunt Aïda assigned him a place in the shade. Now Taaw was eating alone without moving from there, and then leaving for school. But he never once told his mother what was happening to him at his uncle's house.

In the middle of the day, a scorching wind came up. Beasts and humans alike sought rest, as if to store up energy for the rest of the day. Taaw moved away from the shade of the tree to a cooler spot, not far from Aunt Aïda's open window. He began to revise his history lesson ...

'Don't you realize what Yaye Dabo's plan is? She wants Sakhaly to adopt his nephew. That's why she made Taaw come here. There's a school in her area. This scheme of hers will be to the detriment of our own children,' Aunt Aïda was saying. Taaw listened carefully.

'Taaw eats a lot, and too quickly, too. You'd think he never got any food at home,' Aunt Anta said.

'How do you expect him to get enough to eat? Baye Tine gives Yaye Dabo and her three children nothing. He wasted no time using the money he got for clearing out of his house to take a second wife, who's leading him a merry dance. And as you know, in a few months he's going to put in for retirement. That's why Yaye Dabo wants to put this moral obligation on her younger brother and take from our children their due.'

Aïda had said all this in her loud, garrulous voice. Taaw forgot his lesson: he must get up and escape. He was afraid that the rustling of his caftan would give him away. On all fours, he crawled towards the trunk of the doob.

'Ey! Ey … Taaw! What are you doing? That'll bring bad luck! Mother! Mother!' shrieked Oulimata, Aunt Aïda's youngest daughter.

'What are you doing, Taaw, you wretched child? *Kuf mala!*' Aunt Aïda screamed through the window.

Her coarse face crumpled up … ' May the misfortune you are invoking fall back upon you and your family.'

Aunt Aïda suddenly appeared, followed closely by the other children.

They all started berating Taaw for his behaviour which was certain to bring misfortune down on them all. Taaw stood hanging his head, avoiding their eyes.

'Quick, wipe out the marks you made,' Aïda ordered, as she hit him over the head with a wong. 'To whom do you wish death? *Kuf mala*! May misfortune fall back on you.'

The wong sent a needle-sharp pain shooting through him, spreading a burning sensation through the whole of his young body. Taaw was drenched in a hot sweat; his ears were ringing. With a desperate effort of will, he rubbed out the marks his knees had made by walking backwards and using his feet.

The following suns were sheer agony, for Taaw. He was completely ostracised by Aunt Aïda, who terrified him. In her presence, Taaw lost all sense of his own identity. Her hatred enveloped him like a cloak which was suffocating him. Because of his estrangement from his cousins and the pressure his aunt brought to bear on him, he felt his isolation keenly, in his very flesh, in his child's heart. Instinctively, he accepted and submitted to his situation. After he had paid his respects to his two aunts, he would take his place under the doob, and there wait for his food. The two aunts gave him the cold leftovers from the night before. The child had not been on this diet for three weeks when he caught dysentery and ran a high fever.

Yaye Dabo watched over her son. She had to take him into her bedroom, because he was sleeping so fitfully. Her days were spent doing the washing, lavishing care and attention on Taaw, and cooking for Souleymane, Abdou and her husband Baye Tine. Yaye Dabo made a proposal to her husband one morning over breakfast, at the end of her *mômé*:

'Tonight you will be sleeping with your second wife. I would like to bring Taaw in here, into our bedroom ...'

She paused. Sitting on the ground facing the man, her neck and shoulders bent forward, she then said deliberately: 'You can stay with your second wife, until Taaw is well.'

'Is it as bad as that?' Baye Tine asked, after he had swallowed a mouthful of bread and gulped down his tea. His eyes were fixed on a point on her forehead which was covered by the headcloth she wore at night.

'Yes,' she replied, without raising her eyes.

That same day, she moved Taaw into her bedroom and set about ridding his young body of the sickness. Either the Soumaré or the shameless Aminata would take over as home nurse so that she could do her shopping. In his sleep Taaw would thrash about, sweating profusely. He became delirious, and as he tossed and turned, he would deny over and over; 'It's not true! Aunt, I'm telling you that he's lying. Ask Abdouley? ... I am not lying.' This monologue would end in yet more restlessness. Yaye Dabo felt that these words were some kind of warning. What little money she had put aside vanished rapidly on medical expenses. She consulted a 'set-cat', a soothsayer, who told her:

'There is somebody who wishes harm to your son. If you do not protect him ... he is in danger of dying from this ... This child is destined for a great future ... Fame awaits him.'

Yaye Dabo believed him. She sacrificed two red roosters, to remove the *ciat* (evil tongue) and the *bët* (evil eye) which were hounding Taaw. She went to see a great witchdoctor who gave her some *safara*[1] for Taaw. She herself, having returned to her devotional ways, beseeched help from the Muslim saints, from the prophets of Islam and from Yallah. Slowly, Taaw emerged from the world of the sick. He started getting out of bed and leaving the house to sit in the yard. At dawn, Yaye Dabo would lead her son down to the sea so that he could take purifying baths. He let her push his head under the water several times his face turned towards the rising sun. Then the mother whisked eggs over Taaw's head and threw them in different directions. She covered her son's arms and loins with *gris-gris*.[2] She saw her son picking up again, starting to move around on his own, laughing with his brothers, watching television in the Soumaré's lounge. The mother's heart filled with joy every time she heard Taaw's lively voice. The illness had totally transformed him. He seemed to have grown in character; his eyes shone with the lustre of old ivory, and gazed out steady and direct.

One afternoon, when the sun was roughly in its fourth phase, Taaw came to keep his mother company in the enclosure which served as a kitchen.

'I haven't been seeing my father?' Taaw said questioningly in a calm voice.

Surprised by his question, Yaye Dabo stopped her work. She saw Taaw's penetrating look.

'It is your father's time at your little mother's,' she replied.

Taaw stared at her with unwavering eyes.

'Don't look at me like that, Taaw' she said, with anguish and still feeling guilty.

Like a young girl overcome with confusion in her suitor's presence, she lowered her eyes. She was sorry she had lied to him. During the two moons of the illness, Baye Tine had made

* Translator's note: [1] kind of holy waters, blessed by a marabout, used for ceremonial washing. [2] fetishes

a few appearances, only to slip off again for days on end to his second wife. How had her son managed to guess at the estrangement between herself and her husband? At that moment, her gentle maternal tenderness gave way to deep fear. In an attempt to overcome that feeling, blot it out, she said:

'While you were still in bed, your school teacher and two friends came around to see you. They left a message for you.'

Looking sideways towards the entrance of the concession, Taaw watched the people who lived there coming home. He seemed engrossed by his passing thoughts. 'I have to go back to school ...'

'You can tell your uncle and aunts that I'm not very pleased with them. Not one of them have come to find out how you are.'

'Mother, I'm not going to eat at my uncle's anymore.'

The determination in Taaw's voice made it impossible to argue with him. He spoke calmly about what had happened to him with his cousins and his aunts. As Yaye Dabo listened to her son, cries of 'Ah! Ah!' escaped from her ample breast, and in between these exclamations she reeled off the Dabo family tree.

'Now I know why you almost died! They wanted to kill you. Why didn't you tell me? Did you speak to your uncle about it?'

Taaw shook his head, and became withdrawn. There was a long silence.

When the women in the neighbourhood heard what had caused Taaw's illness, they were shocked. They gathered together every day after lunch in the shade of the huts and chattered. Greatly vexed by her younger brother's indifference, Yaye Dabo repeated over and over: 'For two moons the child was on the verge of death. For two moons, my brother, same father same mother, did not even bother to come and see his nephew ... He could at least have sent someone to find out how he was!'

'Maybe he doesn't know about it ... Maybe neither of the wives told him ... If they were wanting to poison his nephew, would they have dared to talk to him about it ...? Calm down,'

Soumaré advised her, lying on her side, her feet sticking out beyond the shade.

'You must go tell those two women a few home truths. I'll come with you if you like,' Aminata proclaimed vehemently.

'You? ... Never,' Soumaré declared, all too familiar with Aminata's sharp tongue. Then she addressed Yaye Dabo: 'Go and find your brother ... If it's just the two of you you can explain everything to him. It's better than confronting those two women in their own house.'

The half-dozen women deliberated about what steps should be taken, what behaviour should be adopted.

'That would be running away, Yaye Dabo. If I was in your shoes, I'd spell out the truth to those two females in front of your brother. And just you see if they'll dare to touch you. With mothers, as with sisters-in-law, you have to spit the truth in their faces ...,' Aminata insisted, supported by three other women.

'My flesh is crawling with shame! To deprive a child of one meagre meal a day ... It is unworthy of any mother,' Yaye Dabo said with restraint.

During that week, Baye Tine resumed his rotations. He returned to his first family without noticing the subtle changes that had taken place in Yaye Dabo, and in his oldest son... Yaye Dabo confided in her husband one night, telling him the cause of Taaw's illness.

'I didn't even know that Taaw had been having meals at Sakhaly's. You know very well that, in your brother's house, Aïda, the *awa*, is the one who wears the trousers.'

Baye Tine's reply deeply wounded her pride in being a descendant of the great line of Dabos. She immediately regretted that she had spoken to him about her brother. Taaw had gone back to school, but he no longer took meals at his uncle's house. He had grown very thin. His marks suffered because of his illness, and he had to repeat the year. Unfortunately, he also lost his bursary.

The holidays arrived. The matter weighed heavily on Yaye

Dabo's heart. She spent restless, gloomy nights. As she thought about it, she could find nothing to justify what the two women had done to her son. And Sakhaly?

She recalled different stages of Sakhaly's childhood. For her parents, it had been a hard struggle. Rumour had it that Sakhaly was a sweet, beautiful baby which a djin mother had swopped for another baby – an ugly scrawny child with legs already crooked, knees as gnarled as the trunk of an old kapok tree, and a huge forehead extending into a misshapen skull which bulged over the back of his neck. From the time that Sakhaly learnt how to walk, his parents were alarmed at how slow he was. Sometimes, when he was alone, he would smile, with a far, faraway look in his eyes, in keeping with the legend of the changeling. At other times, his face would be blank and expressionless. He started speaking late. Then his hump began to form. As he grew older, he became the laughing-stock of the children his age. Sakhaly would run away from them and take refuge in his older sister's arms. In order to shield him from the bullying of the neighbourhood boys, he was sent away to one of his uncles in the north-east to learn the Koran and the tailor's trade. He returned to Dakar as a young man. He aged prematurely, and this made his face look as rugged as the bark of a *cailcédrat*. Once he was installed in his own business with a sewing machine that he hired monthly, he proved to be a master in the craft of scissors and needles. His camisoles, bou-bous, dropped waists and A-lines ... his embroidery work and his innate feel for colours earned him, in women's circles, the reputation of having good taste. He made clothes for women only.

Sakhaly was by now a popular man, and dreamed of taking a wife. He was aware of his ungainly physique, and hid his crooked legs under well-cut garments and fine fabrics. With his overly sensitive disposition, he was afraid to declare his intentions. Aïda Mbaye, considered according to the norms of that country to be of a mature age for marriage, was able to pierce the tailor's shell, and touch his heart. Paying little heed to other people's jeers, she made her intentions plain. They were duly wed. Aïda Mbaye proved to be a perfect wife; she was meek, submissive and docile, and open to her in-laws. She was fertile too, and honoured her husband with two sons and three daughters. Could that be a sign of certain love? When both his parents died in the same year, Sakhaly started clinging to his wife, and distancing himself from his older sister Yaye Dabo, who had a married life of her own to lead with Baye Tine. In his workshop, Sakhaly had a dozen or so tailors in his employment. He was known and admired, a respectable man who had done well for himself. Young divorcees and widows hung about him like flies. Aïda Mbaye, a practical and logical woman, pre-empted her husband by presenting him with a gift.

'I know a young girl who would suit you very well as a second wife. I would get on well with her too.'

Sakhaly, who was on the point of going out, came back to his chair and sat down without saying a word. Aïda Mbaye sat on the linoleum, lower than her husband, surreptitiously watching him. She added:

'You must take this girl. I won't be jealous of her.'

Sakhaly said nothing; he was tempted to question his wife … How had she guessed that he wanted to take a second wife? He refrained from asking questions.

'You go to work … I'll see to everything …'

'You are too kind, Aïda,' he said by way of reply and assent.

Sakhaly went to tell Yaye Dabo about his wife's proposition. Quite some time before Aïda had spoken to him about taking a second wife, Sakhaly had confided in his older sister.

'Now that you're a successful man, you're in a position to take two or three wives, but out of loyalty to Aïda, you should speak to her about it first. I'll take care of it, if you like,' his sister had prudently advised him.

'As soon as I find the right one, I'll let you know.' Sakhaly had concluded the conversation.

Before the month was out, Sakhaly told Yaye Dabo about

Aïda's plans.

Yaye Dabo shuddered.

'Did you speak to her?' she asked.

'No! No! ... She suddenly came out with this, just as I was about to leave.'

Yaye Dabo scrutinised her brother's face compassionately, as if searching for something that might dispel her apprehensions. Aïda had so subtly created this void around her husband.

'Do you know the girl? Where she lives? Who her parents are?'

'Nothing! ... Nothing.' Sakhaly replied without hesitation.

An expression of alarm crossed his sister's face. Without thinking, she crumpled up the hem of her blouse. Yaye Dabo was disturbed by the magnanimity of her brother's wife. She wanted to advise him to refuse this wife-offering.

But she dismissed that idea, thinking, 'He'll only repeat what I say to Aïda. What can that woman's plan be? What is she up to?'

A week after this conversation between brother and sister, Aïda Mbaye came to visit her sister-in-law. She was cheerful and full of smiles, and brought with her some cola and two five-thousand franc notes which she gave Yaye Dabo. Civilities were duly exchanged, and then she brought up the subject.

'*Ahan!* Your brother has spoken to me of his intentions. He is thinking of taking a second wife.'

'Sakhaly has never confided in me about this.' Yaye Dabo was aware of her sister-in-law's duplicity.

'I take your word for it, Yaye. I only wanted you to know, as you are our older sister, that I have nothing against it.'

Yaye Dabo felt numbed by a heavy sadness, which suddenly allayed her anger. 'This woman is cruel,' she said to herself. When their eyes met. Aïda Mbaye added, with a forced smile: 'I know that no wife can welcome this ordeal ... of feeling duplicated. I'll do all I can to help the nieces and nephews to succeed in life.'

After Aïda Mbaye had left. Yaye Dabo simply shook her head in amazement.

When Sakhaly married his second wife, Aïda Mbaye was praised for her generosity, and hailed as a model wife.

Remembering all these things, Yaye Dabo realized that Aïda Mbaye had the lives of her brother, his second wife, and the children completely under her control. Everything was now clear. Aïda was trying either to kill the nephew or to estrange him from his uncle.

Anta received Yaye Dabo, and ushered her into the sitting-room. She was talkative, and bombarded the guest with questions about Baye Tine and the children, but never once did she mention Taaw's name. Yaye Dabo answered evasively, keeping her distance.

'Sakhaly should be home any minute now,' said Anta, bringing the transistor radio in. 'There's a job I must just finish ... there, you can listen to the Imam's sermon. Aïda has gone to a celebration at the neighbours' – it's the fortieth night since their mother died. Everyone knew this woman: she raised three generations... sons, grandsons and great-grandsons.'

Yaye Dabo had to stop herself from saying: 'Now there are only stumps of men left for female meat like ourselves.' Instead she said: 'I heard the news of her death. Quite a funeral, I've been told.'

Yaye Dabo heard Anta saying to Oulimata outside: 'Run and tell your mother that your aunt Yaye Dabo is here.'

Sakhaly came in, dressed in a light-blue boubou embroidered from top to bottom, and a pointed Haoussa headdress.

'Big sister ... Dabo,' he exclaimed, after his *'assalamaleïkum'*.

'Dabo! Dabo!' Yaye Dabo returned his greeting, in a voice whose coldness the brother did not hear.

'Have you been waiting long?'

Sakhaly continued undressing as he spoke. Yaye Dabo watched him. The protuberance at his shoulder seemed larger, bulging unnaturally under the white turki* and the checked

* Translator's note: short-sleeved shirt worn by a man under his pull-over.

Palestinian shawl. Sakhaly hung up his big boubou and ran his right hand over his freshly-shaven head. Sitting on the armchair next to her, he asked after the children and Baye Tine.

'I haven't seen Djibril Taaw's marks. I hope he's moving up to the next class. If Yallah grants me a long life, I will do everything for him.'

Yaye Dabo reeled. Could he really not know what had been going on in his own house?

'*Assalamaleïkum!* Dabo! Dabo!' Aïda Mbaye knelt before her as she gave her greeting.

A feeling of warmth had been re-awakened between brother and sister, but it was cut short by this unexpected arrival.

'Mbaye!' Yaye Dabo in turn greeted her.

Yaye Dabo saw through her sister-in-law's deference the duplicity with which she treated her husband in the presence of a third person.

'I've just been at the home of the deceased, Fatou Diagne – it's her fortieth night.'

Aïda was justifying her absence.

'She was a saintly woman, always ready to help others. May Yallah take pity on her, may he help her, and grant her his divine mercy. We are but passing visitors on this earth. The existence of families and communities is a fabric made up of many threads of life, which are severed by the deaths of the Grim Weaver's Design. Should you go before me, we shall meet on the other side... May Yallah keep us from all evil thoughts, from bearing grudges, and from greed.'

'*Amine! Amine!*' the two women chorused.

Yaye Dabo, feeling glum, answered Aïda in a neutral voice, holding back her frustration and anger. She controlled herself by keeping quiet. Her eyes wandered towards the door, and into the courtyard bathed in light. Aïda too was avoiding Yaye Dabo's eyes, which flashed at her every now and again. Anta and Oulimata brought in the meal: white rice seasoned with dried oysters and thin slices of meat in white sauce.

'Queen of mothers, you cannot tell me that you ate before you came here. Come and sit down.'

Anta invited Yaye Dabo to get up from her armchair. She handed her the fingerbowl in its small plate.

'Cissé, good food is tasted first through the nose, and then on the palate. I will do honour to your cooking.'

The meal, with the two wives present, was conducted in silence. The echoes and sounds of the day rang through the house. Anta, taking up her *mômé*, did all she could to ease the tense atmosphere. From time to time, Yaye Dabo's eyes wandered to her brother, who was eating studiously, like a polite child, his thumb pressed against the edge of the bowl. When the meal was over. Yaye Dabo washed her hands and wiped them with the towel that Anta gave her.

'Let me give you some cold water. We have a new refrigerator.'

'*Jërejëf* Cissé! Thank you, Cissé. I'm not used to water from refrigerators. Could you give me some water from the kitchen?' Yaye Dabo asked, without looking up from cleaning her fingers.

Aïda, half-turned towards the door, called out:

'Oulimata, bring some drinking water for your aunt.'

Anta placed the bowl delicately on the outside of the circle. Oulimata, with one knee on the ground, held the bowl of water out to Yaye Dabo who drank, saying to the little girl: '*Jërejëf doom*' ... Then the cola nut was broken and passed around.

'Sakhaly, when last did you see Taaw?' Yaye Dabo asked, stretching out her legs.

'Djibril? As you know, I am never here during the day, except on Fridays after prayer. Is Djibril perhaps ill?'

'No! I thank Yallah, he is not sick anymore ... Cured. But when was the last time you saw him?'

The commanding tone in Yaye Dabo's voice distressed Sakhaly. He hung his head, and ran his right hand over his smooth-shaven, shiny scalp.

'Sakhaly, you deprived my son of food in your own house. You refused to give alms to your nephew ...'

'What are you telling me?'

'Exactly what you heard, and your wives too. They refused to feed my son. He was given leftovers that no pig would eat. It made Taaw ill for two moons. Two moons! He has now gone back to school … Neither you, my brother of the same mother and father, nor any of your wives has been concerned enough to find out how he was.'

As she spoke, Yaye Dabo was hitting the ground. She thrust her face forward so that she could catch Sakhaly's eyes.

'Yaye, I swear it, on the memory of our father and mother, I know nothing about it. What happened, Aïda?'

Aunt Aïda twisted her upper body around so that she was facing her husband. Not once did she look Yaye Dabo in the eye.

'Nobody in this house stopped Taaw from eating. It's true that once or twice I reprimanded him. Once he was standing out in the yard and started urinating. And when I ticked him off, he was cheeky to me. After that, he started beating the children, so I made him eat alone, to avoid fights. He ate exactly what we were eating. I don't know what he's been telling you … But that's the truth. And Anta and I were just getting ready to come and see you … when grandmother Fatou Diagne passed away.'

Aïda had said all this in a calm, measured voice.

'Queen of mothers, what you've just heard is the truth,' Anta confirmed.

Out of the corner of her eye, Yaye Dabo was watching her brother's face – it looked like an old pestle made of ebony, its ends rounded by domestic use. She knew that her brother was feeling ill at ease, and that he would never dare to contradict Aïda. She felt a surge of pity for Sakhaly, who was no more than a puppet in this woman's hands. She thought of their father: the son had none of his father in him, neither his impetuous character, nor his strong qualities of leadership. Aware of the unrelenting hold that Aïda had over him, she felt sorry for him again. It was because he was her brother that she felt disappointed, forgetting the soul-destroying way in which Baye Tine dominated her life.

Yaye Dabo looked up and surprised her brother trying to catch Aïda's eye. He looked like a child caught in the act of doing something he might be punished for. Baye Tine's indictment resurfaced to her mind: 'In Sakhaly's house, it's Aïda who wears the trousers.'

'Yaye, I want Djibril to come back to this house,' Sakhaly said in a forced voice, ill at ease, like a stranger in unfamiliar surroundings.

'Who was he asking that?' Yaye Dabo wondered, drawing in her legs again.

She turned her eyes to Aïda, squarely seated with her back to the light.

Although a dark halo blurred her features, Yaye Dabo thought she could make out a disdainful gleam in the eyes of the *awa* ... the first wife, meaning: 'In this house, nothing is decided without my consent.'

'Sakhaly, Taaw is now taking his midday meals at the home of some friends.'

'Yaye, is there anybody dearer to you on this earth than me?'

'*Deeded! Deeded**, Dabo,' Yaye Dabo replied, dispelling the obvious embarrassment on her brother's face. She continued: 'Dabo, because of blood ties there is nobody above you.'

'Yaye, you know what I mean,' Sakhaly cut her short, 'I want Djibril to come and live with his uncle. Yallah has given me the means to provide for him as I do for my own children.'

Hearing her brother express this desire so strongly soothed away the rest of the older sister's anger. There was a long silence in the lounge. The cries of children playing outside rang in the air.

'Hasn't the *awa*, who alone is queen of this house, still to say what she thinks?' Yaye Dabo mockingly enquired, while her half-smile said: 'If I like, I can have you repudiated. You tried to kill my oldest son.'

'Me? ... Queen of mothers, it is not my place to decide any-

* Translator's note: 'No, not at all!'

thing. When big sister and little brother get together, the wife and mother of many children is a mere stranger,' Aïda retorted, careful not to frighten off her sister-in-law.

She had realized that Yaye Dabo had the upper hand.

'Queen of mothers ... bring Taaw back to us,' Anta added, supporting whatever her co-wife said.

'I will ask my husband. The last word must come from the men,' she concluded, pleased with her victory, and that she had managed to save face.

Sakhaly stood up, relieved to see the palaver coming to an end.

'I'm going too,' Yaye Dabo said.

At the door, Yaye Dabo straightened the neck of her brother's boubou, and re-arranged the shawl covering his hump.

Far from his wives, Sakhaly gave Yaye Dabo some money before taking leave of her.

A very smoky fire had been put out.

During the days which followed her visit to her brother, Yaye Dabo gave the women of the community an account of the interview with her two sisters-in-law. Soumaré praised her for her family spirit and for her clemency towards Aïda.

'You could have pushed your brother to divorce her,' was the comment of the frail Safiétou.

Aminata, who was involved in a close game of *wure**, grabbed Houdia's wrist and declared: 'If I had come with you, I would have told that pest Aïda a few hometruths.'

'You can speak, but let go my arm,' protested Houdia.

'Yaye Dabo did very well,' added another who was busy mending her children's clothes.

Yaye Dabo, feeling pleased with herself, allowed them all their say.

* Translator's note: *wure*: a game played widely in West Africa. Pips and seeds are used as pawns or men and placed on a wooden board with 14 hollows.

Before school started again, she used some of the money from Sakhaly to buy Taaw new clothes. She never breathed a word of this to her husband. When classes started, Taaw was getting up at the same time as the worshippers going to their Fadjar prayer. For the first few weeks, Taaw used the money he had been given to take his midday meals in a café: a plate of rice with meatballs or fish.

When Yaye Dabo's funds ran out, his diet changed drastically. Sometimes it would be a piece of bread and some chocolate, sometimes dry bread with a packet of roasted peanuts. He would have a drink from the nearest tap and then learn his lessons under the trees at the entrance to the school. He came home at night with a hollow in his stomach. He became known on the bus: the conductor and his assistant would keep him a place. On the bus, he spent the time studying and revising his lessons, especially in the morning. This coming and going between home and school took their toll on the pupil's physical strength, and blunted his mental alertness. Always tired, and fighting off a continual drowsiness, Taaw often arrived late for class; he would not be allowed in, and spent many mornings wandering about aimlessly. In the afternoons, he would try to catch up the morning's lessons by copying out his friends' notebooks. Arriving home at night with an empty stomach, he would then try to double his efforts.

Out of the corner of her eye. Yaye Dabo watched her oldest son. She saw him, all alone, learning and reciting his lessons by candlelight. Her mother's heart filled with loving, comforting thoughts. One Sunday, Taaw stayed in bed longer than usual. She was worried, and asked him: 'Are you sick?'

'No, mother', he replied, burying in the deepest part of himself his most secret thoughts.

During the following months, Taaw, on the verge of collapse, was unable to concentrate any longer in class: his eyelids would grow heavy, and he would doze off. Sometimes he slept outright. He even fainted a few times during break time. His marks for the month, the term, and the whole semester, plummeted lower than the required average. On the day before school broke up the pupils were given their marks and their positions in class. Taaw looked at his report: he had been expelled. At home, he handed the report to his mother.

'You know I can't read. Are you promoted to the next class?'

'No, mother. I've been expelled from school,' he answered as naturally as he could.

The mother gave a piercing cry. She stared at the green card.

'Taaw, what happened?'

Taaw said nothing. He looked away.

'... What am I going to tell your father?' she asked as she clasped her hand to her mouth, staring at her son's face with wide eyes.

Yaye Dabo had always believed that her son would be *somebody*. The radio and television would speak about his interventions and his speeches at congresses, seminars and conferences; they would comment on his travels to the country of the *tubabs*.* She was convinced that Taaw would be a chief, one of the leaders of his generation. That night, Yaye Dabo could find no rest. Cruel images haunted her, and the next day she was morose and downhearted. Going about her household chores, she felt her heart heave with disappointment. Only after her own unhappiness had eased, did she speak to Baye Tine about it. Baye Tine, standing in the middle of the courtyard, fulminated against Taaw.

'When I was your age, I used to walk miles and miles on foot, with nothing in my stomach. I worked so that my mother and father could be happy in their old age. And my father did the same thing for his father, working in the fields. Now that you don't want to go to school anymore, what am I supposed to do with you? You want to be a hooligan, an outlaw?'

Taaw and his brothers listened to their father's bitter outburst. Yaye Dabo took refuge in rigid silence. Baye Tine was giving

* Translator's note: Europeans

way to a strange dark impulse. He himself could not have named this mad burst of molten lava which consumed him and bred in him the desire to hurt others: it was simply a way of masking his failure as a worker. In his sixties, he had taken a second wife with all the ardour of an old man's last desperate surge of life. He wasted no time in giving her two children, in the space of twenty-two months, with a third on its way. Did the bookkeeper in him imagine that the heavy burden of being the 'father of a large family' would secure him an extra four or five years of work before retirement? The country's independence was marching in apace, with the introduction of reforms providing for the replacement, by Senegalese, of former European bosses.

Baye Tine had presented the director with birth and life certificates of his whole tribe and of his two wives, as well as his second wife's pregnancy certificate.

'This might have been common practice during the colonial era, but now you old men must make way for the youth.'

'But look! I've got six kids. I can't support even one of my wives and her children on my retirement pension.'

'You should have thought of your children sooner. I have orders from the board of Administration. I even have to cut back on workers. I can do nothing for you, old man ...'

Until this moment, Baye Tine had had no inkling that he had acted unwisely. Men had always taken second and third wives on the eve of their retirement. Was he not still strong enough to push a joining-plane? to hammer in nails? to work with a saw? ... the wood industry was dropping him when he needed it most. He looked scornfully at the young director strapped into his three-piece suit, and glowering, said spitefully: 'I'm sure your father benefited enough from that clause to feed your fifteen brothers and sisters, and to enable you to study. And if it wasn't your father, it was us, the workers, whose taxes paid for your education.'

The director looked surly and adjusted his tie. Annoyed at having this obvious fact pointed out, he brought the interview to a close.

Barred from an active life Baye Tine devised various personal projects: he planned to have his own workshop, and be his own boss. The idea gave him much joy. But this positive frame of mind was only the echo of a fleeting thought. One, two, three months, and then a whole semester had gone by and he had not picked up his saw or his plane. He lived a life of idleness, spending money, then borrowing to gratify immediate needs. At night, hiding so that no one should see him, he ruined his tools one by one. Sullen and moody, he would strike out at Taaw, Souleymane and Abdou. He often treated Yaye Dabo very badly, in front of the children. When the neighbours intervened, he started beating his wife at night. The next morning Taaw, trying not to look at his mother, would weep bitter tears. The pain he felt was mingled with a feeling of loathing for his father, in whom he saw not dignified old age worthy of respect, but a hateful old man. The only thing that kept him from running away from home, as he had planned so many thousands of times to do, was his love for his mother.

One day, Baye Tine had neither raised his voice at his children and his first wife, nor lifted a hand to them. The pension money had been paid. Peace reigned between husband and wife. Yaye Dabo had prepared a delicious meal, and Baye Tine had feasted like a king. With his back against the bedhead and his arms outstretched he let out a contented belch. The curtain swayed in the gentle breeze blowing in from the coast. Baye Tine thanked Yallah as usual for this sublime moment, which he was savouring with his whole body.

'You must pay for Taaw to go to a private school.'

'Are you mad? Where do you think I'll find the money for that?' Baye Tine replied sharply.

His blood started boiling.

'With your connections, you should at least be able to get him into a workshop so that he can learn a trade. I'm sure that Taaw would have preferred to be *someone* in an office.'

'You've molycoddled that oldest son of yours far too much!

And it's when you get these sorts of ideas in your head, that you women start looking down on manual workers. You only think of material pleasure ... office, cars, air-conditioned bedroom.'

'I was only teasing you, Tine,' Yaye Dabo said, not wanting to listen to words that would hurt her, and afraid that he might start hitting her.

She escaped to the other women in the courtyard.

In the hope of seeing her son furthering his education, Yaye Dabo made enquiries about sending him to a private school. When she discovered what it would cost for one month, a year, her last illusions faded away. She was suddenly aware just how serious their lack of money was, and understood what it means to be poor. Her mother's heart was aching. 'A tree, which will give no shade, bear no fruit for men or beasts! A seed stunted at the time it was sown!' she thought. Through her son, she could see in her mind's eye all the children of Taaw's age, those younger than Taaw, Taaws still on their mothers' backs, Taaws still in the wombs of all women. She could see young people in the township, on squares and at crossroads, and was surprised to find herself asking questions like: 'What future awaits them? What will that future be like?' She could not answer these questions, and she shivered with cold and dread.

In her youth, Yaye Dabo had never been so reflective, or thought so much about herself, her future, the future of her children. Born, raised, fed, looked after, clothed: her whole destiny was mapped out. Her cycle was complete – girlhood, wifehood, motherhood – and now the baton of life was to be passed on to another woman. The memory of her daughter who had died at the age of three came back to her. Death had wiped out all trace of that fleeting life. This peaceful memory was not distorted by grief. It was only life that tore at her with its claws, carving slashes into her existence day after day.

A scorching heat made clothes stick to the skin. The brown asphalt reeked. The flood of taxis painted black and yellow – the range of yellows had exhausted all possible variations of this colour – streamed past at full speed. White sunrays beat down. Men gathered in groups in the shade of the sparse trees along the avenue.

Taaw, optimistic, was making his plans for the future. His meeting with Bachirou had been a good sign. He resolved to put aside some of what he earned to pay for classes. He came to the level crossing. A long goods-train loaded with phosphate was heading for the harbour. The booms were down, and cars, trucks and bikes were lined up on both sides. The bright light played on windows and hubcaps. A traffic officer, spruce in his khaki uniform, helmet visor pulled right down over his tinted glasses, moved about with the fierce look of a warrior.

Taaw looked around and spotted the grey Toyota with the two girls inside, behind a tarpaulin-covered semi-trailer with three half-naked workers perched on top. He was curious to know what it was carrying: was it rice? corn? flour? sorghum? The insistent hooting of a car attracted his attention. He read: Goor Yummbul. The letters were red, bleeding. From this distance the old man was a dark figure waving one arm, calling him closer. Taaw wanted to run away… A pedestrian behind him tapped him on the shoulder.

'Someone's calling you over there.' The two looked at each other.

The way ahead was clear and vehicles started pulling off.

As Goor Yummbul drew level with Taaw, he shouted: 'Taaw, wait for me on the other side.'

The Peugeot left a plume of smoke spiralling in its wake. This unexpected meeting with his sweetheart's father made him feel guilty. As he crossed with the other pedestrians, the same man, dressed in an ash-coloured caftan, repeated: 'The driver of that van said you must wait for him here.'

Again Taaw flashed an angry look at him.

When Astou's pregnancy could no longer be hidden, his friends had teased him.

'Boy! Get away from Goor Yummbul's fence.'

'Boy, as soon as you see a Peugeot, you must jump into the nearest Citroën,' another had added, trying to be witty.

'Hey, boys, we should baptise the first child of the gang,' Mbengue had suggested.

They had lined up together to urinate. Juvenile merriment, general hilarity.

'Taaw! ... Taaw! ...'

Taaw stood nailed to the ground. Aladji Ngom was coming towards him.

There was a halo of sweat marks all around his skullcap; his shirt was loose on his small lean body. Taaw felt intimidated and avoided the piercing look aimed straight into his eyes.

'Do you have nothing to say to me?'

Taaw said nothing, holding the trousers more tightly under his armpit, and tapping them.

'My daughter Astou is expecting a child, and you are the father ...'

Was he telling him? Asking him? His authoritative tone threw Taaw, and he did not know how to respond.

'Will you answer me?'

A beggar approached them, holding out his open hand.

'I've already forked out alms for today,' Aladji Ngom said harshly to him.

'What about you, my boy, have you given yet today? Don't forget that Yallah will pay you back, in the world hereafter, with three times what you give today to a *miskine*.'

Taaw turned his back on him. The tramp went up to a woman passing by.

'I'm waiting,' persisted Aladji Ngom. As Taaw still did not reply, he went on: 'You think I don't know what you're scheming? You think the hedgehog act* will get you anywhere?...

* Author's note: hedgehog act: this burrowing animal neither digs nor constructs its own home. Protected by its sharp quills, it inhabits the first burrow it comes across. The original inhabitant either leaves the burrow or stays there and is suffocated by the hedgehog, whose burrow it has now become.

Goor Yummbul launched into a diatribe against the youth of today. A passer-by took him for a father lecturing his grown son. With abuse and accusations being hurled at him, Taaw reacted. Looking scornfully at the old man, he lifted his arm, and interrupted him.

'Ey Pa, have you ever once seen me in your house? And don't speak to me in that tone, I'm not your son. All the boys in the neighbourhood "know" your daughter Astou.'

This was a blow to Goor Yummbul's pride, which at the best of times was easily ruffled. Taaw's bitter words had stunned him, and he remained speechless for some seconds. In a fit of frustration, he grabbed Taaw, who pushed him away with all his might. Like an old goat in a raging fury, Aladji charged. Taaw, being the more nimble of the two, ducked out of the way and punched him in the side. The seventy-year old bent over double before collapsing to the ground. People ran up to separate them. Taaw grabbed the trousers and briskly strode off, leaving the crowd behind him.

Taaw felt liberated from the awe that Goor Yummbul used to inspire in him. He had found relief in action. He skipped around like a boxer in the ring, and laughed self-assuredly. A woman was watching him as he imitated a fight. He calmed down and walked on again, turning to look back at the woman who stood staring at him.

As he reached the string of cheap eating-houses, the smoke from frying meat and fish mingled with the heavy smell of peanut sauce and reeking palm oil, and the tart aroma of chilis and rice, arousing his hunger. Apart from the pilfered fritters, he had had nothing in his stomach since early that morning. With seventy-five francs in his pocket, he asked himself what he could afford. He walked past the food stalls in the shade of the filaos* and bought two ladles of fatty meat soup.

'Ey, woman, let me have this chili,' demanded a chap next to Taaw, pushing his bowl over the pot.

---

* Translator's note: conifer or shrub of the casuarina family, found in the coastal regions.

The swarthy woman, who had a thick, shiny face and big white eyeballs, half-heartedly gave it to him.

'Let's share it, brother,' from somebody behind.

Taaw took a seat on a Rufisque stone which a customer had just left. People were eating, squatting on their heels by themselves or in groups of two and three. Taaw relaxed and began to think. Now that he had a job in the harbour, he was sure to find a ship so that he could take himself off to Europe, where he would pursue his studies. He had not relinquished his ambition to become a computer scientist. And Astou? He convinced himself that he was not the father of the child she was carrying. After all, how could he be sure? Once he had left and gone far away, he would not need to justify himself. As he ate, he gazed into the distance, unconsciously playing with a dry filao apple.

'Who would like some water?' the water-carrier cried, putting his bucket down.

A dozen plastic bottles were floating in some water together with a piece of ice.

'One bottle,' ordered the person nearest to Taaw, an elegantly dressed man.

On his wrist, he sported a large gold watch. He quenched his thirst with small sips straight from the bottle, taking care not to spill on his caftan.

'Your turn, *petit*.'

Taaw had a long drink. Water trickled down his chin and dripped onto his anango. He put down Baye Tine's trousers.

'Thank you,' he said.

'That piece of rag there, is it for sale?' asked the man, picking up the trousers with one hand while with the other he passed the bottle on to the next person. First, he examined the trousers feeling the cloth. 'Good cloth... Fashionable cut. These aren't yours,' he concluded, affecting a connoisseur's air. 'I'll give you three thousand-franc notes.'

'You, you must pay me for my water,' clamoured the vendor, who had retrieved his empty bottle.

The guy was the bragging type. He looked the hawker up and down, took out a wad of banknotes, then dug deep in his pockets for two coins to give him. The men around stared greedily at the money.

'So *petit*, will you accept three notes?'

'Five,' answered Taaw, standing up and taking back the trousers.

'*Alcati-y*! *Alcati-y*! Cops! The cops are coming,' a chap, breathless, gave the warning.

The well-dressed man dived hastily into a passing taxi. The taxidriver almost crashed into a car coming the other way. In no time at all, the open-air restaurant had emptied completely. It was like an anthill crushed by a huge paw, as its patrons scattered.

Taaw, still carrying the trousers, headed towards the township.

A second time, the muezzin's call to the prayer of Takusan came over the air through the loudspeaker.

When Taaw reached his territory, the place of the 'Jobless', reggae was blaring out full blast. The music came from a loudspeaker attached to the fence. On the dusty road some young people, all boys, were dancing, moving with the music. A small group sitting on the ground was playing belote-bridge, while others were feverishly intent on a game of draughts. The two in charge of the galley were making mint tea, which the gang drank every day.

'Taaw!' one of them, with a small face and a speckled lower lip, called out, making room for him on the bench with the other supporters of the draughts players.

'Have you found any work, boy?' Mam Ass asked, as he left the dancers and came up, sweating.

'The same vague promises as usual!' Taaw sat down with his legs turned outwards, leaning his elbow on the trousers.

'Taaw, don't give it away,' warned Daffé, the player facing him.

'But I haven't said a thing,' Taaw protested, looking around at the others as though calling for witnesses.

'Boy, I know you. You always do it. Just check how thick Toumani is. He doesn't even crown. Play, boy.'

'Don't let him mess you around, boy,' the one with the marked lip encouraged him, slapping Toumani gently on the back.

Toumani swung around and looked questioningly at Taaw.

Daffé shouted:

'Taaw, shut up!'

The music stopped.

'Boy, put on the Toure Kunda,' Mbengue shouted from the middle of the improvised dance floor.

'Oh, you've just got here!'

Taaw took the steaming glass of tea. Sipping the hot liquid, he carefully took stock of the position of the draughts. He reacted excitedly.

'You're so thick, Toumani. You arsehole ... no one could be more stupid ... I don't believe it. This is too much ...'

'Too late,' Daffé yelled, wasting no time in swiping three draughts off the board.

'I thought he'd move over there,' Toumani justified himself.

'Unbelievable! You're an arsehole, a total arsehole ... even there he would have taken you and crowned.'

Everyone was talking at once.

One of Astou's younger brothers tugged at Taaw's arm and said: 'Astou's waiting for you at the main road.'

'How did she know I was here?'

'I told her ... I saw you come in.'

'Finish my glass.'

The child drained it in one gulp and ran off.

Noises were dying down as the day drew to a close. The evening breeze blowing from the south-east was dispersing the cloud-banks in their layers of different colours stretched out across the sky. A vast basin carpeted with moss lay at Astou's feet. Groves of filaos, palms and coconut trees, upright trees and slanting ones, were dotted around the edges of the valley. Sand dunes the colour of salmon, like young women's lips, shivered as the wind breathed gently over them. People were walking along the paths. Neither the flesh-colour of the sky and the flight of birds towards the setting sun, nor the scene she had before her was touching Astou's thoughts. An aesthete would have said that girls are not sensitive to beauty.

She caught sight of Taaw, and a powerful feeling of love flooded her heart. She wanted to take Taaw in her arms... like this morning, when his thumb was moving up and down, stroking her whole body. As she looked around, the sight of passers-by destroyed this sudden surge of feeling.

'You haven't sold the trousers,' she said, relieved, her voice gay, her eyes laughing.

'No,' Taaw replied coldly, watching a child pulling along a reluctant goat.

'Have you found work?'

She looked at Taaw, her hands held expectantly, waiting for some gesture from him.

'I'll know tomorrow. Why did you want to see me?'

'I've got a prescription from the midwife. I've been to the chemist. I need seven thousand francs for the medicine.'

'Where do you think I'm going to find that kind of money? ... Do you want me to steal it?'

Astou was distressed by the unexpected harshness in Taaw's voice. 'Taaw,' she said pleadingly ... 'Taaw, don't speak to me like that.'

'Where will I find seven thousand francs?'

'Apart from you, who can I go to?' she said with tears pricking her eyelashes.

'Here, go and sell the trousers.'

'*Muq! Muq!* ... Never. Your father's trousers ...'

She pushed Taaw's arm away. Imploringly, she said, 'You must be able to borrow from your friends. This morning I gave you the thousand francs that I had. And there's no way I can ask my father for that money ... You ...'

'Yes, I saw your father today. He wanted to hit me.'

'My father ...' she interrupted.

'... Yes, yes. You and him, you take me for a fool. Astou, I'm not your child's father, you're just trying to pin it on me.'

'Taaw!'

This sound was torn from her, rather than cried out. She clasped her hands to her stomach. Staring at Taaw, her mouth half open, tears flowed from her eyes.

'It's true. Go and find a father for your child somewhere else.'

A wound of this kind cannot be measured. For how long did she stand there, removed from herself? Passers-by noticed this pregnant girl standing motionless, her eyes gazing far off above the trees. Tears were running down her cheeks, and falling onto her chest between the cloth and her skin.

She started at the sudden kick in her stomach. She acknowledged it, then sniffed, straightened proudly, and headed for her father's house.

It had been a good day for Yaye Dabo, in spite of its bad start. It was the second day of her *ayé*, and the women who owed her money had come to fix up their accounts and buy condiments. She did her shopping; two kilos of Siam rice – an economy rice, easy to digest – a quarter of a litre of groundnut oil, and two average-sized gilt-head fish. As she went about her household chores, she was working out in her head the price of meals for two days. She would have enough money to see her through the next three days.

At midday, she had given Souleymane, Abdou and their father lunch. After his fish and rice, Baye Tine prepared to take his usual siesta. Yaye Dabo had not forgotten her Taaw, and had made a snack for him. 'Will he have eaten? ... Where? ...' Being out of work was difficult for her son, and he was becoming taciturn. What worried her more, however, was the violent animosity between father and son. When she joined the other women in the shade of Soumaré's shack for the rest she took there every day, she forgot her cares a little. There was washing on the lines; mats and household containers were out in the sun to dry. Aminata, wearing an old candy-pink nightshirt over her full bust, was burning bedbugs with a lighted torch. The torch's flame licked at the bed base, whose metal springs had been mended with wire.

'The bedbugs! I'm the only one in this house who gets them,' she was grumbling.

'Buy some insecticide,' advised Houdia, who was breastfeeding her three-month-old baby.

'My foot! ... That stuff only makes them fatter,' Aminata replied as, with a single movement, she pulled up the strap of her shirt: 'Look at this bitch stuffed full of my blood. This very sun, you are going to hell.' She held the torch to the insect. 'Tomorrow it's my *mômé*.'

'So if it's your *ayé*, let your husband fight the bugs. Then he'll buy you a new bed with a foam mattress instead of a straw one.'

'Houdia, you haven't "blacked the ear" of your baby yet. I have to compete with my co-wives. I'm the fourth ...'

Aminata stopped what she was doing, and counted on her fingers. She turned her head away from the smoke, and said in a loud voice.

'Three, six, nine ... I've been waiting for my husband for nine days. And if he can't get any rest with me, he'll run me down and tell me how wonderful my co-wives are.'

'Keep him on his toes,' another one broke in, shooing away the hen with her two pairs of chicks.

'Exactly, I'm getting ready now to receive him properly. When the poor wretch gets to me, he's in a bad way. I fix him up well the first night. But the other nights, I make him pay for my troubles. I milk him dry. And even when it's siesta time, he does it. Nobody eats my rice just to go to sleep. I refuse to fatten him up for the others.'

They laughed, enjoying Aminata's spicy sense of humour.

'Every bed has its bugs. If you don't talk about yours, no one will know about them,' Soumaré said to Yaye Dabo, who was sitting a little to one side.

Soumaré was being deloused, her head resting in her daughter's lap.

'Mother, there's a cluster of nits in here.'

The conversation divided into two.

'What do we want from life? Just what we need to live? To feed our children? Bring them up? Have you noticed how many of them there are in the houses and the streets?' Yaye Dabo said plaintively, more to herself than in reply to the Soumaré.

'I've stopped thinking about all that. I leave those worries to my husband,' answered the Soumaré. And to her daughter: 'Yes! Just there! Yes, scratch hard. You're doing very well ... *Ahan! Ahan!*'

The girl was scratching her mother's scalp with her fingernails; Soumaré was sighing softly. Yaye Dabo ventured a quick glance at her. Her eyes slid along the woman's thighs. She was clasping her knees, and vigorously rubbing her toes together.

'Yaye Dabo, Yallah has put men on this earth. And on earth, he will see to their needs,' retorted a neighbour, after a surreptitious glance at Soumaré.

The latter smiled, re-arranged her disarranged loincloth, and turned onto her other side.

'If Yallah is really going to help you, you have to put something into it yourself.'

'The Koran says so,' added Soumaré, wiping away the spittle at the corners of her mouth.

'It's their "tomorrow" that worries me. When they come of age, these young people won't know how to till the land, or weave, or smelt iron. And tomorrow, they'll be in our places ... mothers and fathers .... This tomorrow worries me ...'

Yaye Dabo fell silent. She would have liked to explain herself better. Her questions brought about a sudden intense silence. The sound of the rooster's beating wings as it chased the hen broke the silence, and they resumed their chatting. Aminata turned the bed over. With her thumb, she wiped away the bead of sweat falling into her eye.

'Yaye Dabo, you are saying things that we, as women, do not like to hear. The tomorrow of our children, you must ask the men about that. Look at the township! Who knows where it starts? Or where it will end? All the ethnic groups in the country can be found here mixed up together. Famine and drought do not only drive whole families from the villages, they also destroy and dislocate the community, and break up family unity. Urbanisation and the development of commercial centres push the have-nots out into the townships. And here, amongst us, we have some of the better-off poor, as well as the most destitute poor. Tomorrow, it is from these townships that the leader, or the leaders, the real ones, will come.'

They had all listened to Aminata.

'Aminata, where did you learn all that?' asked Yaye Dabo, inwardly reconciled with Aminata.

Suddenly Aminata undid her loincloth, and shook it violently. She was wearing blue panties.

'That bitch is climbing all over me to go I don't know where ...'

Picking up her torch again, she angrily thrust the lighted end into the ground.

'Give my regards to your kin in hell ...' Then, turning to Yaye Dabo, she continued: 'Yaye Dabo, this is the township area, between the city and the country. None of us women wants to return to the bush. For me, the days in the bush are over,' she concluded. And she launched into another subject. 'Do you know what happened this morning. That stuck-up Oulimata Yandé was thrashed to death by a maid. She was rushed to hospital. The maid was taken to the police and she's being charged with violence. But will the people who judge her tomorrow take into account the reasons why she did it?'

'It serves Oulimata Yandé right. She never did anyone a

favour,' said Houdia.

The conversation turned to more general matters such as the ever-deteriorating relations in the neighbourhood.

The call for the Tisbar prayer heralded the setting of the sun.

Yaye Dabo woke Baye Tine so that he could do his duties as a Muslim. She proceeded with her ablutions, and carried out her ritual alone. She never missed a prayer. In her entreaties, she implored Yallah to place his blessed hand on Taaw. When she had finished her devotions, she went back to join the group of young wives.

After the Tulkussan prayer she got down to preparing the evening meal. She repeated to herself Aminata's words: 'Tomorrow's leader will be born among the children of the townships.' Already she could see Taaw as one of these heroes. Thinking about Taaw brought to her mind the girl he had made pregnant.

'At least he's a real man,' was her one consoling thought. She remembered the mornings before and after Taaw's circumcision, when she had seen him having an erection. 'I've got a rooster.' All she had to do was watch over her hen. She laughed to herself, hearing joyful music in her head. She felt flattered that Taaw had made Goor Yummbul's daughter pregnant. A respectable, well-off family, which would raise their position in society. For nights on end, she anticipated the visit from Astou's mother ... or at least from her emissaries, sent to negotiate. With the help of Soumaré and Aminata, she would receive them. There would be two of them.

'Soumaré ... our steps have brought us here, to demand compensation,' the younger one would declare, so that the other one would be able to drive the point home.

'Compensation ...? Compensation, did you say? In what way are we guilty of harming anyone ...?' Soumaré would ask, feigning surprise.

'Ah! ... Ah! ...' the younger of the two would say, pressing her lips together, her eyes lowered.

She would then take up again, with a more sceptical tone in her voice: 'Ah! ... You do not know what it is that you are guilty of?'

Aminata would make a soft noise in her throat. She would take some time before speaking.

'What is known but not said on the engagement day, will be known on the day of the divorce. We are listening to you.'

It would then be the older messenger's turn to speak.

'It is still our plant. We have sown it, nurtured it.'

'Was the plant promised?' Soumaré would ask.

'Yes,' would be the reply from the younger messenger. 'And you have badly wronged us. You son Taaw has "deceived" our daughter.'

'We can understand that this must be an unpleasant situation for any mother to find herself in,' Soumaré would say. 'We must first speak to the accused. Then we will decide what standpoint to adopt.'

'All we are asking is an admission of paternity.'

'Ey! Ey! What? Are we not good enough to have your daughter as a wife?' Aminata would demand, holding herself upright.

'Everything in good time.'

'The sheep which is sacrificed on the day of the baptism, will be served that night at the nuptial meal.'

'We will speak to our daughter.'

'Taaw!' she exclaimed in surprise. The thread of her monologue was cut short.

She collected herself. 'Come and sit down!' she invited. 'I kept you a snack. Are you hungry? I'm sure you've had nothing to eat?'

She watched her son's face, trying to pierce through the stern mask forming around the boy's mouth, in the first wrinkles, in the torments etched on his brow.

'I'm not hungry, Mother. And I didn't sell the trousers. I've been promised work for tomorrow.'

'*Inchalahoo!* ... *Alhamdoullilahi!* ... I knew that Yallah would never abandon you. You have never done anything against my mother's heart. Yalla has granted my wishes ... *Alhamdoullilahi!* ... *Abdou! Abdou!* ...'

'*Nââm*,* Mother.'

'Where is Souleymane?'

'He's in the street, Mother,' Abdou replied, coming out of the lean-to.

'Ey, boy,' Taaw murmured, putting his arm around his brother's back.

'Ouch!' groaned Abdou.

'He's really in pain after the beating he received this morning,' said Yaye Dabo, untying the knot of her loincloth.

She counted out some coins and said to Abdou: 'Go and get some cigarettes for your big brother, and buy yourself some sweets.'

Taaw had taken the child's wrists.

'I'm sorry, boy. I'm going to tell father not to touch you again. You're a man now. On Saturday night we'll go to the movies. How would you like to come and see a good film with me?'

Abdou nodded his head, and went off.

'Don't start giving him ideas. His father has the right to punish him if he does something wrong.'

Taaw said nothing. He hung the trousers on the wash-line and went back into the little room. Yaye Dabo was watching him. She re-arranged the legs of the trousers before returning to her job of cooking the evening meal.

As the minutes went by, the house came alive: laughing, children crying, *assalamaleikums* and *aleikum salams*. The shadow of the shacks, steadily lengthening, was preparing to drape itself over the remaining outlines and shades. Women, or their daughters, were clearing away the day's washing. The only thing left hanging on one of the lines – Yaye Dabo's – was Baye Tine's pair of trousers.

'Yaye Dabo', Astou greeted, putting down her bundle. Souleymane was with her.

'Souleymane, who is this lady?'

'She's looking for Taaw, Mother.'

Yaye Dabo, sitting on the bench in front of her fire and her pot,

* Translators note: Yes

frowned.

'Which Taaw are you looking for?'

'Yaye Dabo, I am looking for your son, Djibril Tine, whom everybody calls Taaw.'

'Who are you? ... Where do you come from?' Yaye Dabo asked, her whole body filled with apprehension.

'Yaye Dabo, I am Astou Ngom, the daughter of Sohna Diène and Aladji Ngom.'

Yaye Dabo stood up heavily. She looked up, down, and her gaze finally lighted on Astou's face, in which one could see that she was pregnant. Their eyes met across her stomach.

'Why are you looking for him?'

The question had come out naturally.

'He's the father of the child I'm carrying,' Astou replied without difficulty.

Yaye Dabo had had a traditional upbringing; modest, and used to expressing things more delicately and subtly, she was disarmed by Astou's direct replies. Embarrassed, she moved closer to the girl, until she was touching her stomach, with mixed feelings of tenderness and pity. She examined the texture of her skin between her breasts and around her ears. A golden jewel hung from her ear, and she wore a thick gold chain around her neck. 'A parting gift from her mother,' she said to herself. The presence of this young girl-mother filled her heart with joy. To hold her grandchild in her hands! Just thinking about it already gave her immense satisfaction.

Astou looked down, trying not to stare at Yaye Dabo too much.

'Taaw! Taaw!' Yaye Dabo called.

They both looked towards the lean-to.

'Taaw, my father has thrown me out,' Astou said as soon as she saw the young man.

'I'm telling you again, I am not your child's father,' was Taaw's retort, when he had taken the cigarette from his lips.

Then he made to go back into the lean-to. Astou held him back.

'Taaw, how dare you say that to me? Who gave you two five-hundred franc notes this morning, so that you wouldn't have to sell your father's trousers ...? These trousers, here, on the line. Do you want me to remind you of all the places you have taken me to?'

Taaw did not notice Astou's sharp look. A long, and interminable silence followed.

The fleeting joy of a moment before had vanished. Yaye Dabo was overcome by a feeling of infinite sadness. She both admired and detested Astou's quick repartee.

'Taaw!' she said without moving, convinced that her son was not telling the truth.

'Mother, this girl is lying.'

'You're the one who's lying. And you know it.' Astou flashed this at him, standing squarely in front of him, her jaw thrust out arrogantly, her eyes fixed on his.

'Mother, I'm telling you again this girl is lying.'

'Taaw, be a man.'

Yaye Dabo's slap came with a crash across Taaw's cheek. She was stunned by the violence of her action and looked around, frightened.

This violent outburst of his mother's left Taaw rooted to the spot, motionless. He felt a warm liquid in his mouth. He touched his finger to the corner of his lips, and looked at the blood.

The women crowded around. Aminata whispered to Houdia, who had her baby on her back:

'At least she knows what she wants, that one.'

'*Ndyesan!* Her father has disowned her.'

'Who is her father?'

'Goor Yummbul.'

'*Ndyesan!** One chooses neither one's father nor one's mother.'

And a series of comments on the times we live in, broke out. Aminata started speaking:

'Yallah gave woman a strong back to carry all her children, whether they're illegitimate or not. Who among those who

* Translator's note: Alas!

govern us, spiritually, or temporarily, can tell us who is or is not a legitimate son?'

'Ey! Ey! Aminata ... Think about what you say. One day you'll have your tongue cut off.'

'What is going on here?' Baye Tine demanded, as he came bursting in.

They all moved away.

'Nothing! ... Nothing, Tine,' Yaye Dabo answered him. And then to Soumaré: 'You can look after this girl until tomorrow. The person she is looking for will come for her then.'

The two women exchanged an understanding look.

'Come this way,' Soumaré invited.

Astou obediently took her bundle and passed in front of Baye Tine.

'You, who are you?'

Baye Tine's question came like an explosion.

'Baye Tine, she's my visitor.'

Baye Tine scrutinized Astou from top to bottom and then made her turn around. They faced each other.

'Tell me, who are you?' Astou cast a glance at Taaw as if to ask: 'What must I answer?' Taaw took two steps as his father was repeating the question.

'Answer me, who are you?'

'Baye Tine, I am the daughter of Aladji Ngom and ...'

'You're pregnant by the doings of the good-for-nothing. I heard at the mosque that your father had thrown you out. And as for you' (this to Taaw), 'do you really think I'm going to keep you in my house and feed you, you and your bastard child?'

'Don't say that again,' Yaye Dabo implored.

'Quiet!' bellowed Baye Tine, menacing and aggressive.

He turned to Taaw: 'I'm going to shake out my trousers. You'll be cursed forever, you'll be the least among those of your age.'

The husband and wife both rushed for the trousers on the line. Yaye Dabo grabbed them.

'Give those to me ... They're mine! Give here, I tell you!'

'You have no right to wreck this child's life,' Yaye Dabo said as she aimed the trousers at Aminata.

Aminata caught them and made to throw them to another woman.

'Just you wait!'

Taaw held back his father's raised arm, and said: 'If you ever touch my mother, I'll kill you.'

'Taaw, don't hit him,' Yaye Dabo interrupted.

'Hit me! Hit me ...! Break another of my teeth.' Baye Tine was pushing his chest against Taaw. 'I'll throw you out of my house, together with your bastard child.'

'Taaw, I beg of you, don't touch him ... for my sake ... I'm asking you ... As your mother.'

Taaw released his father's arm. He gave his mother a searching look, then picked up the bundle and took Astou's arm, to leave with her.

'Taaw! Taaw, where are you going?'

'Let him go. Let that ungrateful brat of a son go.' Baye Tine restrained Yaye Dabo, who was struggling against him, calling after her son. 'Let him go. If he comes back to this house, I'll repudiate you.'

'Repudiate me ...?'

Yaye Dabo had often heard this word, and each time it had made her stomach feel hollow, and filled her with fear. The word was more terrifying, more deadly, than being whipped. She had paid everything with her body, stifling her rebelliousness, swallowing her inner thoughts, so as never to be sent away, never to be discarded like an old used rag. She had married with a pure heart, thinking only to fulfil her life's duty as a wife and mother. As a wife, and a mother, she had not expected some miracle to transform her life into a paradise. But she had hoped one day to enjoy the fruit of a mother's labour, and occasionally, to share a laugh with her husband.

'Repudiate me!' she cried out again.

She was an upright, clear person, submissive and obedient by nature, but with unlimited strength of will. As a mother, she had the courage and suicidal spirit of the hen who faces a predator about to take her chicks from her. The patience and self-restraint of this stocky, average-sized woman acted as a curb on those impulses which it was not good to let free.

'Repudiate me ...'

'If you let him return, I will repudiate you.'

She pushed Baye Tine away with such force that he fell down. Yaye Dabo grabbed the trousers from Aminata.

'Well, it is I who repudiate you, and in front of these witnesses too. Leave this house. Keep your trousers, they're all you have here. In front of the men you act the part of husband. But when it's just the two of us, you are as limp as this old cloth. In this house, anything that stands upright is thanks to me. You no longer have a wife here.'

She stood firmly in front of the man, who was sitting on the ground. The women, drawn by Yaye Dabo's sudden revolt, stood speechless.

'Don't touch me!' she shouted at the Soumaré, who had placed a hand on her.

'Dabo, one does not humiliate one's husband like this in front of one's children.'

'And him, he can do it to me in front of my children? ... No ... A husband who gives you nothing to eat, nor any clothes to wear, and curses your children, what use is he? Baye Tine is no longer my husband, neither before the men, nor before my children.'

She stepped insolently over Baye Tine, an act violently condemned in Wolof society, particularly when done by a woman. From the threshold of the concession she surveyed the scene, empty without Taaw and his sweetheart. She turned back again, bitter.

Baye Tine stood up sheepishly. With his trousers slung over his shoulder, he made for the exit, followed by the women's mocking eyes.

'Tchim,' Yaye Dabo taunted him, when they passed each other.

'The time we have been waiting for will come, when beauty and goodness will be inside us. And we will know them and love them, by looking inside ourselves.'

'Ey! … Ey! … Aminata! Aminata, stop saying things we don't understand,' said Houdia as she and the other women returned to their chores.

In front of her pot, Yaye Dabo's face was calm and peaceful, a result of the strong control she had over herself. She refused to see the world around her through the eyes of other people. The events of the day filed cruelly past in her mind's eye, and then the thousands and thousands of humiliations she had suffered in her life rose before her. She lifted the pot lid. A cloud of steam billowed out and formed a halo around her head. She slipped the vegetables in, and took out a few coals which she quickly buried, to save them for later.

'Souleymane! Souleymane!'

'Yes, mother.'

He came to her, with Abdou at his side.

'Go and find Taaw for me! His pals must know where he and "his wife" are … Souleymane, you must tell them they can come and live at home. They can have the lean-to.'

'Mother, Abdou and me, where will we sleep if they come back?'

'In my room, Souleymane. Now quickly go and find Taaw! I'll wait for you for supper.'

The mother's face shone with loving compassion as she watched her sons going off. As she cooked the meal, she had the sense of being in control of her own fate. She knew that by opening her home to Taaw and "his wife", she was turning the community against her: it would be a defiance of the society's matrimonial mores. Already she could hear the various reproaches which would not fail to plague her.

After the meal, with Souleymane's help – Abdou was suffering from the effects of the caning he had received that morning – she converted the lean-to into a bridal chamber, and put out a snack. After they had watched television at Soumaré's, the two little boys came to their mother's room. They fell asleep in no time. Yaye Dabo was listening out for the slightest noise. She would sleep for brief moments, and then suddenly start awake from dreams which pounded her with her guilt. In her dreams, she was pleading her cause, trying to defend what she had done.

In front of all the neighbours, Soumaré was accusing her: 'Yaye Dabo, you cannot condone your son's *nekale** with this girl, under your roof. Already, you have dared to repudiate your husband ... and a Muslim woman has no right to do that.'

She answered: 'Soumaré, you are too sensitive to the words of men. This girl, who chased her out of her father's home? And her mother, where is she? ... with the girl's father.

'Who refused to give shelter to his own daughter? What evil have these two children done? Worse things are happening in society, far more hateful and blameworthy than what these two young people have done.'

'You can't live ignoring the judgements of others.'

'If the others want to kill me, I will ignore their judgement.'

'What I'm saying is for your own good. All fingers will be pointing at you.' said the Soumaré, retreating. 'I am on your side, Yaye Dabo. It's the men who make the marriage laws, and they are the first to break them.'

Yaye Dabo emerges with a start from a heavy sleep. The room, drenched in darkness, is filled with Abdou and Souleymane's soft, regular breathing. The sound of whispering voices coming from the lean-to fills her heart with an almost child-like joy. She can feel the presence of Taaw and Astou, just as long ago she had felt Taaw in her stomach. It is as though a gentle, caressing wave is sweeping over her. 'They've come back just like little children who come to snuggle up in their mother's protective arms,' she says to herself.

Moved by a sudden impulse, a compelling urge to speak to them, she sits up in bed .... Then she restrains herself, listening. The sound of their voices is broken by silences. These silences disturb the mother. 'Are they going to leave again? ... to fly away?' ... she wonders, frightened. In the dark, barefoot and

* Author's note: concubinage

with her arms stretched out in front of her, she gropes her way past obstacles, so as not to wake the two boys sleeping on the ground. She pulls the door open slowly and peeps through: the dim, flickering light of the candle standing on the floor falls on the door of the little room. Yaye Dabo can only make out her son's tall shape. Astou is half hidden by the door, and only her back and legs are in the light. A patch of soft light glows on her breast, lighting up her necklace, which gleams and sparkles with flashes of gold.

'I can't be late for my first day at work,' Taaw keeps saying, tearing himself away from the girl.

'Taaw, don't leave me ... I'm frightened,' she says in a trembling voice.

'Don't leave the house.'

'Your father will throw me out. I'm frightened, Taaw.'

'You don't have to be frightened of my father. My mother told us to come back. She knows what she's doing ...'

'Taaw, don't leave me. You're all I have, do you understand that?'

'I swear to you, on our child's head, that I'm coming back to you. Go back to bed now. We mustn't wake my mother.'

Taaw softly pushes the door closed.

Yaye Dabo feels happy to hear her son speaking to "his wife" in this way, and proud that she has given birth to a man worthy of his name. In her head is the sound of soothing music. She goes out into the courtyard, having no desire to go back to bed ... The shadows of the night drawing to a close cast an uncertain glow. Stars are still shining in the sky. The warm dawn brings her the conviction that never again will she be a woman of the past. Strangely, she feels that she is putting into motion a whole new world.